DOUBLE VISION

CODE NAME 711

F.T. BRADLEY

DOUBLE VISION

CODE NAME 711

HARPER

An Imprint of HarperCollins*Publishers*

ISBN 978-0-06-210440-3

Typography by Lissi Erwin
13 14 15 16 17   CG/RRDH   10 9 8 7 6 5 4 3 2 1
❖
First Edition

To Tyne and Nika

PROLOGUE

HAVE YOU EVER WATCHED A REPORT ON THE news and wondered what *really* happened? And I'm talking about the true events, not the made-for-TV version.

Like this January, there was a big presidential ball at the White House—costumes and all—and supposedly there were rats in the East Room. They had to evacuate the place. It was panic time! "Rats at the White House," they called the story.

The truth? It was a total lie. There was a rat at the White House, all right, just not the kind with whiskers and a tail, if you know what I mean. Nobody is supposed to know what really happened at the presidential ball. It's the stuff they think the public (that's us) can't handle.

But I've got the scoop. It's a top secret case, and it involves the president of the United States.

Ready?

PLACE: JUST OUTSIDE SAM'S HOUSE
TIME: SUNDAY, 5:41 P.M.

Here's how it all went down.

1

YOU KNOW THE DAYS WHEN EVERYTHING is going perfectly? I was having one of those that Sunday. I'd just creamed Sam and Daryl at Racing Mania Eight, I was on track with school stuff (or close enough anyway), and Mom was cooking dinner since she had no classes and only one shift at the hospital that day. I would be home before six to set the table, so extra dessert for me. Life was good.

I rode my skateboard away from Sam's house, going extra fast down the hill. But when I saw the black sedan at the end of his block, I slowed. Wondered if maybe my gut was wrong.

Maybe this was some guy who was really into tinted windows. Maybe I should cross the street (safety and all that) and speed up. There was a plate of spaghetti and meatballs waiting for me. Chocolate cream pie for dessert. Just because there was a black car parked on my expected route home didn't mean that Pandora had come for me.

But then the driver's side door opened. A black lace-up shoe stepped on the pavement—a woman's shoe, but not the girlie type. Sensible footwear, made to catch a bad guy. Secret agent shoes.

Agent Stark got out of the car and gave me a little nod. And I knew my gut was spot-on: *Pandora was back.*

I got off my board and carried it as I walked toward her. "Hey, Agent Stark. You must be here for my mom's spaghetti dinner."

"Afraid not." She scanned the street, but the place was quiet. "Why don't you get in, and I'll drive you home."

Now, ordinarily it's a really bad idea to get into someone's car, even if you know who they are. Any kid knows that. And my board was just fine for getting me where I needed to be.

But this was Pandora's Agent Stark. If she came all the way to Lompoc, California, to talk to me, something had to be up. I had that familiar sense of dread and excitement in the pit of my stomach as I got into the dark sedan.

I put on my seat belt and tucked my board in the back of the car. "If you think I'm coming with you to pretend to be Benjamin Green again, you can forget it." Ben Green is this junior secret agent who looks just like me. On my first mission for Pandora, I took his place when he went missing.

"I wish I could forget it." Agent Stark sighed and put the car in drive. She doesn't really like hanging out with kids—in fact, she doesn't really like anything as far as I know. Agent

Stark is one of those humorless government agent types: brown hair always in a bun and never a smile. "But Albert Black sent me."

"Why didn't he come himself?" I asked, even though I knew he was Pandora's head honcho.

"He's meeting with the president." Agent Stark stopped at a yellow light.

"President of what?"

"The United States of America."

My jaw dropped. "President Griffin *herself*?"

"Why is that so surprising to you?" Agent Stark gave me an irritated glance. "Pandora is vital to national security. Black and President Griffin are going over mission strategy."

I almost asked her what the mission was but then stopped myself. The last time I joined Pandora, I was chased by bad guys in Paris and ended up jumping from an airplane. I know secret agent life sounds really exciting, but almost getting skewered by the Eiffel Tower is not. "I thought you had Benjamin Green for this."

Agent Stark hesitated. I could see she was thinking about what to say as the light turned green. "He's on another case. In fact, all of Pandora's other teams are on vital missions. We're it."

"So you need Agent Linc Baker, huh?"

"That's right. We need your special skills."

"And it's just me, no Ben."

"Yes." Agent Stark pulled over at the end of my street. "Can we count on you?"

"What's the case?"

Stark reached to the backseat and grabbed a blue folder. There were CLASSIFIED stamps all over it. "Here." She tossed it on my lap.

I opened it and got confused pretty quick. I learned from my previous run with Pandora that there's lots of boring paperwork and forms with mumbo jumbo no one outside the government gets.

"Flip to the printout of the email," Stark said.

I did and read the page:

TO: Mustang
FROM: Dagger
On schedule for Thurs @7 termination of POTUS and family.
Weapon will be retrieved in 48. The Washington is within reach.
Retain cover.

Huh?

"I have no idea what this means," I said. "What's POTUS?"

"That's what we call the president." Stark glanced to her rearview mirror, like someone out on Sam's street could be following us. "The email was intercepted and reported in the Presidential Daily Brief—it came straight from the director of National Intelligence."

"Something's planned for Thursday. *Termination.* Then it hit me. "Dagger wants to kill the president!"

Stark nodded. "And her family."

From watching TV, I knew President Griffin had a husband and a daughter, Amy, who was roughly my age. "Don't they have Secret Service and the FBI or whatever to protect them?"

"They do," Stark said. "But cutbacks have left them with reduced manpower. And this is serious enough that the president personally requested Pandora's help. There's a costume ball planned for Thursday at seven, in honor of Celebrating America's History Week. We think that's when Dagger plans to strike."

"Why did the president request Pandora?"

Stark shifted in her seat. "I don't know. Albert Black is keeping this case close to the chest." She sounded a little annoyed. "I'm sure we'll find out more once we get to Washington."

"So I'm supposed to just come along, without knowing what the case is."

"It's a few days in Washington, DC," Agent Stark said. "A vacation on us. You'll be back on a plane by Friday. And I'll even call your school so you won't get in trouble."

Something told me it wouldn't be that easy. But then I was reminded of this big history test I had on Wednesday. It was a killer, on the Revolutionary War and the Founding Fathers—and I'd studied for roughly five minutes so far.

This could be the break I needed. "I'll do it," I said. "I want just one thing." I told Agent Stark about the test.

"Consider it done. I'll get you an A."

"Make it a B-minus." I reached for my skateboard in the

back and opened my door. "Can't have Mom getting suspicious." *Mom and Dad.* "Wait—how am I going to explain this trip to Washington, DC, to my parents?"

"Say it's a science fair."

"I stink at science."

She cocked her head, like she was thinking. "Spelling bee?"

I shook my head. "Even worse."

"Is there *anything* you're good at?"

Racing Mania Eight. Skateboarding. Eating ten fries in one bite. Getting into trouble. "Not really."

Agent Stark shook her head. "I don't know, Linc. You're a smart kid."

"I am?"

"Creative, too. So make something up."

2

I SHOULD PROBABLY MENTION THAT making stuff up is something of a specialty of mine. Sure, I get into trouble sometimes, but I have good reasons. Some-one had to prove to Mr. Finch that if you put more Mentos in a Coke bottle, the soda sprays higher. And I've talked my way from a D to a C-minus a few times already, so when Agent Stark told me to make something up, she knew I had the chops to pull it off.

Need a story? Leave it to Linc.

But for some reason, I couldn't think of one excuse that would convince Mom and Dad to let me take off to Washing-ton, DC, for a week. As I chomped down on my third juicy meatball at dinner that night, the lies weren't coming to me.

It was kind of alarming, to tell you the truth. Like Spider-Man losing his superpowers.

"You're quiet tonight, Lincoln." Mom smiled at me from across the table. "Everything okay with your friends?"

"Sure. Yeah."

Grandpa muttered something cranky next to me. He thinks playing Racing Mania Eight on the Xbox is a waste of time—typical attitude of people who don't know the skill it takes to level up twice in an afternoon. Grandpa is more into old-school entertainment. Like five-thousand-piece puzzles and watching ancient movies with gangsters in them.

Mom squinted. "There's something going on. . . . Wait—did you get a bad grade?" Her smile dropped.

"No, no." I had to tell them something. Come up with some story before I lost my chance at chocolate cream pie. "Actually, there's one thing," I said, thinking maybe I could just wing it. "It's a trip."

"A field trip?" Dad lowered his fork. My last field trip didn't go so well, so he had reason to be worried.

"No, more like an overnight excursion," I said. Good spin, even if I do say so myself.

"During a school week?" Mom raised her eyebrow. I swear, she's like a human lie detector. "I thought you had a history test."

"This is for history, actually. It's a trip to the White House." Technically, that wasn't even a lie.

Dad lowered his fork. "You're not talking about the Junior Presidents Club, are you?"

Huh?

Mom grinned from ear to ear. "Is that it, Linc?"

Junior Presidents Club—what on earth was that? I stuffed a forkful of pasta in my mouth to cover my confusion.

"What's this Presidents Club?" Grandpa asked. Thank goodness for Grandpa, because I was flying blind here.

"There was a report on the news about it a few weeks ago. It's a short internship for promising young students," Dad explained to Grandpa, who looked like he thought it was just a load of nonsense. But then that was Grandpa's general expression, even when you told him the sky was blue. "President Griffin hosts a group of middle schoolers for a week so they can watch the government at work. The kids get to shadow staff members, tour the White House—it's a really great opportunity. On completion of the program, they get a certificate personally signed by the president."

Suddenly, I had six eyes on me as I swallowed my pasta.

Let's face it: I couldn't have come up with a better story myself. So I went right along and nodded—this Junior Presidents Club sounded like just the ticket.

Mom smiled wide. "Why didn't you say something sooner?"

"I guess I was waiting for dessert," I fibbed.

Mom gave me the last meatball. For dessert, I had two extra-large slices of chocolate cream pie. After a really long and boring story from Dad about how he once made it to the spelling bee quarter-finals, we cleared the table. And I was back to feeling life was perfect.

But things were about to go downhill—fast.

3

PLACE: DAD'S CAR

TIME: MONDAY, 10:33 A.M.

STATUS: CRAMMED IN THE BACKSEAT

THE NEXT DAY, I GRABBED MY BACKPACK with Dad's compass clipped to the side, my skateboard, and enough clothes to last me for a week in Washington, DC.

"Now who are we meeting at the airport?" Dad asked from the driver's seat. Grandpa was riding shotgun, and I was crammed in the backseat surrounded by boxes of car parts.

"Her name is Agent Stark." I pushed a box of spark plugs aside to buckle my seat belt.

"*Agent* Stark? As in government agent?"

"Extra security," I said, hoping that sounded believable. "You know, since I'm going to the White House and all."

"Huh," Grandpa muttered from the passenger seat.

"White House, President Griffin, my foot."

Dad shook his head. "How 'bout you just trust your grandson for a change?"

"Yeah," I said. Grandpa was messing with my mojo here. Big time.

Dad got all quiet as he exited Highway 101. "It *is* a little strange, Linc," he said after a few minutes. "Why the short notice?"

"A spot opened up. Last minute, you know," I said. Just a few more miles and we'd be at the airport.

But Dad was beginning to sound like Mom. "Shouldn't there be some sort of permission slip to sign? It all seems . . . fishy." He turned left at the airport sign.

A box of oil filters banged against my elbow. "You know, I don't have to go if you don't want me to," I said. Sometimes you have to pull the old reverse psychology trick. Only as a last resort, because this one can backfire if you're not careful. "I'm sure they have a waiting list of kids who want to be in the Junior Presidents Club."

"No, no," Dad said quickly. He parked and we all got out. "I just want to talk to someone in charge. That Agent Stark— I'm sure she can explain things."

"Nonsense," Grandpa muttered as we walked inside the building. Shut up, Grandpa!

Agent Stark stood near the reception desk. Her face tensed up when I introduced her to my dad and Grandpa.

Dad shook her hand. "Linc told us all about you and your program."

"He did?" Agent Stark looked confused, but only for a

millisecond. The lady was used to lying, so I hoped she'd just roll with it.

"The Junior Presidents Club," I said quickly.

"*The Junior Presidents Club,*" she said slowly. "Of course. We're delighted that Linc could join us at the White House on such short notice."

Grandpa squinted, studying Stark. He's really into crime shows, History Channel stuff on mobsters and the FBI. If it involves crime, Grandpa is all over it. "She's bona fide," he said, pointing at Agent Stark's feet. "Look at the shoes."

We all looked at Agent Stark's boring lace-ups, which I took as a good diversion to move stuff along.

"Well, I guess we need to catch our flight, Dad."

"Sure, yeah." Dad seemed convinced by the shoe business, and Stark got him to sign some paperwork, and blah blah. A few minutes later, they were on their way.

Stark and I checked in (me under Benjamin Green's passport, which was weird), flew the wobbly little plane to Los Angeles, and after an hour layover with a quick greasy burger for lunch, at one thirty we were off to Washington, DC.

Before settling in for a nap, Stark gave me another blue folder with CLASSIFIED stamps all over it. I opened it and saw it was full of stuff I was supposed to study during the flight. There was a picture of the president and one of Amy. The first daughter had shoulder-length curly blond hair, and smiled at the camera with a twinkle in her eye. She looked nice.

Behind the pictures there was a map of the White House, a list of staff names, the president's schedule, and blah blah.

The papers had me nodding off after less than ten minutes.

So I watched the in-flight movie instead—it was a PG-13 action one Mom wouldn't let me see. Then I played some basic video game on the system. By the time I won for the eighth time, the plane was descending.

Once we taxied, I rubbed my face, stretched. And realized:

The folder was gone.

This was bad. I looked to see if maybe it had slipped off my lap, checked under the seats and around the empty spot next to me. But no blue folder.

"You okay?" Stark asked. She was going to kill me.

"Um, yeah," I lied.

The pilot turned off the seat belt sign, and there was the rush for the overhead bins around us. Guys in business suits were getting their carry-on luggage, and other passengers had their duty-free bags; one even had a ridiculously big teddy bear. I grabbed my backpack from under the seat in front of me.

Then I saw something that made me freeze. A lady with long brown hair stood in the aisle with her back to me, a red bag slung over her shoulder. Peeking out the top of the bag was something blue.

My blue folder—I was sure of it. She stole my file!

"Hey, lady!" I yelled, but she was already headed toward the plane's exit.

Stark pulled my arm. "What's going on?"

I pointed to the lady just as she got off the plane and

disappeared from sight. "That lady stole my folder!" I tried to push past the people in the aisle but just managed to get clocked by some guy's oversized carry-on suitcase.

Stark popped up behind me. "The case file?" she hissed in my ear.

"Yes," I hissed back. Finally, the line of people moved, and I tried to resist the urge to push other people aside to catch up with the lady. I got off the plane and ran into the arrival hall.

"Wait!" Stark called behind me.

But I wasn't about to stop. I rushed past the clusters of passengers, guys in business suits checking their phones. And I saw the lady up ahead. She was run-walking toward the escalator at the far end of the arrival hall.

One of those golf cart things zoomed toward me, and I had to jump aside. The guy driving gave me the stink eye. When he'd passed, I looked up—no brown-haired lady.

But then I saw something blue on the floor.

My folder. I rushed to pick it up and riffled through the pages.

Stark came up behind me.

"It's all there," I mumbled.

Stark brushed some loose strands of hair away from her face. "Where'd she go?"

I pointed to the escalators. "She's gone. I'll bet she's a spy or something," I added in a whisper.

"Welcome to Washington, DC, city of spies and lies." Stark glanced around, looking for other spies, probably. Then she pushed me in the back. "Come on, we need to get out of here."

I tucked the folder into my backpack. "What did that lady want?" I asked Stark as we walked toward baggage claim. "Why did she steal my folder? And how did she even know we were on the plane?"

"I don't know," Stark snapped as we walked to our baggage claim spot. "All I know is that we're calling attention to ourselves, and that's not good. So just drop it, okay?"

"Okay," I mumbled. Still, I glanced around to see if the spy lady was getting her luggage. But she wasn't around.

Stark got our suitcases, and by the time we walked outside, I'd decided to forget about the lady thief.

But I shouldn't have. Because I'd meet her again, and she'd mess with a lot more than just a blue folder.

4

PLACE: THRIFTY SUITES MOTEL

TIME: TUESDAY, 7:58 A.M.

STATUS: SLEEPING

IT TURNS OUT THAT THE WHOLE PRESI-
dential assignment wasn't that fancy after all. The motel
room was small with a cheesy painting on the wall, and the
place smelled like someone bathed it in bleach. But after our
long travel day, I honestly didn't care about anything. After
my head hit the flat pillow, I was asleep in less than a minute.

And I didn't set the alarm. So when the phone rang that
Tuesday morning, I was kind of confused at first, since I was
sleeping so hard. "Huh?" was all I managed to croak.

"It's Agent Stark."

I looked at the alarm and saw it was exactly eight o'clock.

"Get up," Stark said, "and meet me in the lobby at eight twenty-five sharp. I want to be at the White House by nine."

I blinked, but my eyes felt like someone had tossed a handful of beach sand in my face. "Linc!"

"The White House." I cleared my throat. "Sure. No need to yell at me, you know."

"I'll see you in twenty-five minutes."

The lobby of the motel felt like a cold shower, with the harsh lighting and the outside air blowing from the revolving door that didn't stop turning. The place smelled of burnt coffee and cheap pastries.

Agent Stark was eating a sticky roll when I got to the lobby. "You're late."

It was eight thirty. "Only by five minutes. And it's three hours earlier back home, you know." I yawned.

Agent Stark handed me a couple of plastic-wrapped cinnamon rolls. "Eat in the car."

I took the rolls, thinking Mom would be disgusted if she saw this sad excuse for food. She'd have a twenty-minute lecture on how bad preservatives are for kids, and a brochure to go with it.

Stark was all business. I wondered if she'd even slept, since she was wearing the same dark suit as yesterday, and her hair was still in a bun. The lady was a machine. Me, I hurried to catch up with her through the motel's revolving door, buttoning my coat.

"Where's our ride?" I asked Stark's back.

"Away from the entry." She waved to the side of the tall brick building. "We need to keep a low profile." That explained the Thrifty Suites accommodations. But as much of a bummer as the motel was, our ride was impressive: a black SUV, chrome wheels, tinted windows. I stopped on the sidewalk to admire how shiny and cool it was.

"Now this is more like it," I said to Agent Stark.

"Get in. You're drawing attention," she said, glancing up and down the street. But nobody was noticing us—they were all too busy getting to work, or wherever it was they were off to.

I got in and sat on the shiny black leather upholstery. I used my teeth to open the pastry packaging and looked down at the spotless floor mats. "Are you sure I can eat in here?" I asked Agent Stark.

"Someone will clean up after you." She got in. "Now remember: You're checked in as Benjamin Green."

"Sure, yeah. You know, you match the car," I joked as I took a bite of the cardboard roll, pointing at Agent Stark's black suit. "If you paint your face black, no one would ever know you were here. You could be a ninja."

Agent Stark ignored me, but I was pretty sure I caught a hint of a smile. She tapped the dark glass window that connected to the driver's portion of the SUV. "Let's go." Once the SUV moved, she handed me a cell phone. "Here's your Pandora phone for this mission. We all have the same kind—please don't use it for personal calls."

I took the phone. "How about my parents—can I call them?"

Stark hesitated. "Just keep it short. You need to be reachable at all times."

I tucked the phone in my pocket. "So what is the mission, exactly?"

"I don't know yet." Stark looked uneasy. "I haven't spoken to Black in two days. He's not picking up his phone." She sounded panicked, which was very much unlike Stark.

"Why not?"

"Never mind," Stark said, composing herself. "We'll simply go to the White House. I'm sure it'll all be clear once we get there," she added, not sounding sure at all.

So I just sat back and looked outside, watching the cars zoom the opposite way. And with each passing car and building, I felt more uneasy. Even Agent Stark didn't know what was going on. That couldn't be good.

Because Black was hiding something. My gut knew it. That, or those plastic cinnamon rolls were talking.

Agent Stark seemed to sense I wasn't feeling the assignment. She tried a smile and said, "It'll be fine, Linc," then looked away. For a secret agent, she sure was a lousy liar.

The SUV pulled up to a black metal gate. It opened like magic, and the driver followed an asphalt driveway. A couple of squirrels chased each other up a tree. I saw a white building up ahead, but it looked nothing like the White House.

"Where are we?" I asked Stark.

"At the White House." When she saw my confusion, she added, "We go in at the West Wing entrance. That's where most of the day-to-day business gets done and where the staff meets."

The driver stopped at a tiny guard building, where he showed his badge to a lady. We then drove on to an overhang in front of the white building.

Agent Stark reached for the door handle but stopped herself. "Remember: You're not some tourist here." She leaned closer, and I could smell the overly sweet motel pastry on her breath. "So please, *act like an agent.*"

"I know." She didn't have to be so cranky about it.

"Let's go," Stark said, getting out of the SUV.

I followed, leaving a trail of crumbs on the upholstery. There was a reason Dad never let me eat in the car.

Stark was already walking up to the entrance, but I took a moment to look around instead. And between the trees, there were those giant white pillars you always see on TV. The ginormous porch that I knew overlooked the lawn, even if I couldn't see it. I had to blink a few times to make sure what I saw was real.

I was at the White House!

TUESDAY, 8:55 A.M.

"LINC, COME ON!" AGENT STARK CALLED.

I followed her through the glass-paned double doors, inside the West Wing, where two guys in suits used metal detector wands to check us. A gum wrapper in my pocket made it go off, which set us back almost ten minutes—they were really serious about security.

Once we made it past those guys, a short-haired lady in a blue suit motioned for us to follow her.

We came into a room with old oil paintings in gilded frames on the wall. There were several sitting areas with antique red chairs and cherrywood coffee tables—not that we were invited to sit down or anything.

"Can you state your purpose, please?" the lady in the blue suit asked Stark.

"I'm here to see Albert Black," Agent Stark said, sounding nervous. "He's with the CIA."

The lady gave her a terse smile. "Can I see your identification, please?"

Agent Stark looked confused as she handed over her badge. She was about to say something when her phone rang. "Black! I've been trying to get hold of you for days," she hissed, turning away. Stark listened for a minute, then hung up without saying good-bye or anything. She turned around and said, "Gregory Wilson is expecting us."

The lady nodded and took off for a minute. When she came back, she motioned for us to follow her. We went right, through a door and down a hall lined with more old oil paintings, portraits of historical people and battle scenes. Then we got to another door and took a left down yet another hall. We passed doors along the way, but all of them were closed.

Once down that hall, we went right, where the lady took us outside. We walked down a portico with white pillars to our right and a fancy-looking rose garden beyond. I was pretty sure I'd seen the president stroll this way on TV—too cool, huh?

"Follow along, please," the lady said when she realized I was trailing.

"Stay close," Stark hissed in my ear.

Like I was going to go anywhere—there was some tall guy in a suit with one of those earpieces, following close behind. As if bad dudes were going to pop up at any second.

At the end of the portico, we went inside again. And in

that hallway, we were met by a bald guy with a friendly smile.

The lady in the suit gave him a nod and went back the way she came, along with the tall agent.

The guy extended his hand. "I'm Gregory Wilson, the chief usher. But you can call me Wilson; everyone else does." He shook Stark's hand first, and she introduced herself.

"I'm Linc Baker."

"It's a pleasure." The guy had a monster grip. "I wish I had time to give you a tour." Wilson turned to Agent Stark. "But there's been a development, so you both need to come with me for a meeting. And we have to move fast."

We followed the guy through the doorway behind him and down a big hall. Then we took a quick left, toward the kitchen. Or at least I assumed that's where we were going, because there was the smell of fresh bread and something sweet baking, like cake.

"So who are we meeting?" I asked.

Wilson gave me a quizzical look, like I was supposed to know. "Why, the president, of course."

6

TUESDAY, 10:15 A.M.

I WAS GOING TO MEET THE PRESIDENT OF the United States! I felt a little clammy all of a sudden. And I secretly wished Benjamin Green could see me on this awesome mission.

"Where are you taking us?" Agent Stark asked Wilson as we followed him down a flight of stairs and into the basement. The ceilings were low. There was no art or anything on the walls this time. "Seems like we're leaving."

We stopped in front of a heavy wooden door, tucked away to the right of the stairway.

And Wilson said, "We're heading to what's called the clubhouse."

"A clubhouse, seriously?" I said.

Wilson smiled. "I think it might've been John F. Kennedy who named it, but who knows? The clubhouse is a meeting place the president uses when he or she doesn't want any eyes or ears. You're about to see one of the White House's best-kept secrets." He opened the wooden door with a key.

There was a smaller stairway that smelled a little like wet dirt. It led to a landing and another door. Wilson pulled out an old key that looked a lot like the one Grandpa uses to lock his old behemoth of a desk back home.

Pausing before it, Wilson turned to face us. "You can't tell anyone about this place, ever. Agreed?"

Agent Stark and I both nodded.

Wilson unlocked the door and said, "Welcome to the White House tunnel."

I blinked to adjust to the lights along the walls while Wilson locked up behind us. "A secret tunnel? No way!" I laughed.

"This passage goes back to when the mansion was rebuilt after the fire of 1814," Wilson told us as he led the way. "Over the years, our presidents have used it to move in secret. It's a bit of a walk to the clubhouse, I'm afraid."

About ten minutes later we got to a heavy metal door. "We're right under the Herbert C. Hoover Building," Wilson said, using another key to unlock it.

"That's it?" I said. "No infrared laser-beam security system that scans your eyeballs?"

Wilson shook his head as he opened the door. "Sometimes, simple is best."

Beyond the door was a hallway and to the right, a metal door with an exit sign on it. Straight ahead, I saw an elevator. To the left, there was an open door. We walked into a stone-walled, windowless sitting area. President Griffin sat in a comfortable-looking club chair at the far right of the room, next to Albert Black.

And standing near the wall, arms crossed, looking all smug, was the guy I hated most: Benjamin Green. My blood boiled in an instant. This was supposed to be *my* case! I felt like going over there and smacking him with my skateboard—not very nice, but I couldn't stand the guy.

Why was he here? I glanced at Stark, but she didn't even look my way.

Ben gave me a death-ray stare. The only upside? He seemed to be as mad as I was. "Baker?" he said, spitting the words. "What are you doing in DC?"

"I could ask you the same thing—you're crashing *my* case!" I was ready to get up in his face, but then remembered: The president of the United States was right in the same room. I had to be cool.

"If I had told you he'd be here, you wouldn't have come," Stark whispered. She pulled me back with her left hand and extended her right. "I'm Agent Angela Stark." She shook President Griffin's hand. "This is Lincoln Baker."

I shook her hand, feeling kind of weird. I mean, she was the president! Of the United States! You had to be impressed by that.

But I couldn't focus on how amazing it was that I was

meeting President Griffin. I felt Ben's annoying presence, and I had to bite my lip to keep from exploding.

"Are you twins?" President Griffin asked, her eyes moving from me to Ben and back to me again.

"No!" Ben and I said at the same time.

"We're not even friends," I said before I could think.

"The resemblance is really remarkable," President Griffin said to Albert Black.

"None of the other government or spy agencies know about these look-alikes," Black said. "They're our best-kept secret—a major asset on this mission."

"I imagine so," President Griffin said.

Benjamin Green, an asset? My foot. But I knew better than to argue with the president.

We got settled in on a chunky sofa that practically swallowed me whole. Ben sat on the edge, like he was ready to go into action any second. On the stone walls there were old paintings of landscapes and portraits of people I didn't recognize. The White House sure liked its old art.

"Let's get started," Albert Black said. But before we could, Wilson had us turn off our Pandora cell phones and put them in a basket. I guess they were worried we'd take pictures or record the conversation or something.

"Yes, let's begin." President Griffin smiled, but she had that same worried look Mom gets when I'm in big trouble. Worried, and a little scared. "Before we start, I need the assurance of everyone in this room that what is discussed will not go anywhere." She looked at Albert Black.

Like I told you already, Black is the head honcho at Pandora. He's a big guy with a voice that sounds like an avalanche. He likes to wear loud shirts, and I never know if he's going to give me a pat on the back or lay into me for something I did. "Pandora is as secure as any team gets," Black said.

President Griffin glanced at Wilson. "You came highly recommended. But I still would like each of you to confirm your utmost discretion."

"Yes, ma'am," Ben Green said, saluting like the president was his drill sergeant.

"You have my word," Agent Stark added.

All eyes were on me. "What?" I was still trying hard not to be mad about Ben being there.

"You need to tell the lady that you'll keep your mouth shut," Albert Black said, giving me a dark look.

"Who am I going to tell? Nobody would believe me anyway." But then I said, with two fingers in the air, "I won't tell anyone I was here, scout's honor and stuff."

That got me a little laugh from the president. "I know how you feel, Lincoln. Sometimes all this security feels a little silly." Then her face got all serious. "Unfortunately, secrecy is my only hope now. There's been a new threat." President Griffin handed Agent Stark a piece of paper.

Stark gasped—only for a second, but it was obvious that whatever was on the paper shocked her. "Was the note mailed in?"

"I found it on my desk an hour ago," Wilson said softly. "Whoever wrote this was able to get inside the White House and inside my office."

Stark handed me the paper, and I quickly read the note:

Dear Madam President,
It is time for your term to come to an early end.
Thursday, 7 p.m., you and yours die.
This Washington is invincible.
Sincerely,
Dagger

Ben pulled the note from my hand and read it before passing it back to the president. "Is there some sort of code in there?" he asked.

For once, Ben and I agreed. "Yeah, what's the talk about 'this Washington'?" I asked. "And didn't that intercepted email also mention something similar?"

President Griffin's hands trembled as she folded the note. "Dagger—whoever he or she is—plans to kill me and my family. Thankfully, my husband is in the UK for an environmental summit and we can keep him safe there. But my daughter, Amy . . ."

"Since the note was left on my desk, we can assume that this person has to be someone who can move freely about the White House," Wilson said.

"A mole, or more like a dirty rat," Black grumbled.

"Not to question your thinking, President Griffin," Agent Stark said, "but why bring in Pandora?"

"The mention of Washington in the threats made us

think we need Pandora." President Griffin glanced at Wilson, then Albert Black. "We believe it's about an artifact. A special coat. The coat has . . ." President Griffin was searching for words. "It has certain properties. Powers that if used by the wrong people could be devastating."

I knew what this was, so I said, "It's a Dangerous Double."

7

HOLD UP, YOU'RE SAYING—WHAT'S A
Dangerous Double? It's a twin of a real-world artifact, only the double has powers that would be dangerous if a bad guy got control of them. During my first case in Paris, we had to track down this double of the *Mona Lisa* that could be used to hypnotize people and turn a crowd into an ugly mob. Dangerous Doubles are bad news.

"You're right, Lincoln," President Griffin said. "The reason I called in Pandora is because Wilson here told me the agency specializes in finding Dangerous Doubles."

"So what does this coat do?" I asked.

"During his time as commander in chief of the Continental Army, George Washington fought in battle for years,"

Wilson said. "Washington was shot four times but survived, even when a horse was shot and killed right from under him—twice."

"Wait—this is *George Washington* we're talking about?" I asked. It was all a little too weird. "As in, our first president?"

"The one and only," Wilson confirmed. "At first, Washington assumed that he was just lucky. But then he inspected his coat and saw it was still in one piece—the bullets had only charred the fabric slightly where they bounced off. He realized that his coat had special powers. Washington and his colleague Major Benjamin Tallmadge tested his theory and found that the coat makes whoever is wearing it invincible. You can't be killed while wearing it—it is the ultimate armor."

"It seems like the Dangerous Double could be of good use in battle, ma'am," Ben said. The guy had a point—invincibility was a nice perk for anyone, especially during the Revolutionary War.

"George Washington was a puritan at heart," President Griffin said. "Am I right, Wilson?"

Wilson nodded. "He worried that whoever had the coat would have an unfair advantage in battle, and George Washington was a man of principle. Plus, you can imagine what could happen if the coat fell into the wrong hands. Who knows, we might have lost the Revolutionary War."

"But the coat is still out there," I said.

"You're right, Linc," Wilson said. "George Washington couldn't destroy it—the coat makes you invincible, after all, so it's invincible, too. Knowing he couldn't destroy the

Dangerous Double, Washington hid it instead."

President Griffin said, "I'm hosting a costume ball this Thursday at seven, to honor Celebrating America's History Week, with hundreds of special guests, foreign dignitaries, and diplomats attending. I'm afraid a lot of them will be wearing Revolutionary War costumes—including coats just like the Dangerous Double."

"Then it would be difficult to spot our enemy at the ball," Ben said.

The president gave him a sad nod.

"So that's the threat: This bad dude wants to kill you and tons of other people at the ball," I said. "But he'll be wearing the coat, so he'll be safe. Wait—he doesn't have the Dangerous Double yet, right?"

"Not as far as we know." President Griffin sighed. "The message has me worried that he or she is close. We've got to find it first."

Black passed around a picture. "This is George Washington's coat, one that's on display at the Smithsonian. It was a very dark blue, with cream trim and gold buttons. The double looks just like it."

President Griffin added, "I've been told the coat is in good shape, and unless you look close, you won't spot where the bullets bounced off it."

"And with this coat, the bad guy would get out unharmed," Ben said. Thanks, I already pointed that out.

But I wasn't going to have him rattle my cage, so I asked, "Why don't you just cancel the ball?"

"The perpetrator would simply pick another place and time," Agent Stark said softly. "If someone wants to do something, they'll find a way."

"Copy that," Ben added. "We know when and where the enemy will strike. This is a position of advantage."

I hate to admit it, but Ben was right: At least now we knew the when and where. We just needed to figure out who was behind it all.

"My life and my family's safety depend on you all." President Griffin rubbed her hands together. "I need to know who the mole is among my staff. And most important, I need you to find this Dangerous Double. Before my nemesis does."

Wilson gave us back our phones and whisked President Griffin away right after that conversation. She was already late for some briefing—places to go and a country to lead. She followed Wilson into the hall, and there was the metal clank of the door a second later.

Albert Black told us that they'd leased one of the offices on the fourth floor of the building—like Wilson said, we were underneath the Herbert C. Hoover Building. It's about three blocks long, and there are all these government offices inside the place. There's also the National Aquarium in the basement and the White House visitor center on the north end.

"Let's go upstairs, and then we'll hash out a plan," Black said. He had a key to access the elevator. We got off on the fourth floor and went down a hall to gather in a cramped conference room.

I was beginning to feel a little nervous. These Pandora missions were dangerous—and this time the president and her family's lives were at stake. That history test wasn't looking like such a big deal anymore.

Albert Black clapped. "Okay, everyone. Have a seat. Time to get to work."

"Yessir." Ben almost jumped to attention.

"You can drop the whole soldier-ready-for-duty act now," I said as we all sat around the table. "The president is gone. And I wish you were, too."

Ben gave me an irritated glare.

"Kids, *kids*," Albert Black said with his rumbling voice. "Save the fighting for after we're done with this mission. In case you haven't noticed, we don't have much time here." Black looked to Agent Stark. "What's your take?"

"Well, first off, I wish you'd told me from the beginning what this was about." Stark looked angry and a little hurt. "Where are you even staying—I thought we agreed on the Thrifty Suites?"

"We're at the Bergdorf Hotel," Black said. That sounded like a serious upgrade from the Thrifty.

"That's nice," Stark said. I could practically see the smoke coming from her ears. "I didn't even know we had a base of operations in this building—I just showed up at the White House West Wing this morning like some idiot!"

Black didn't seem bothered that she was mad. "Presidential orders. I couldn't tell anyone, including you." He made a motion across his lips like he was zipping them up. "Get over it, and let's get to work. What's the game plan?"

Stark nodded but still had a dark look in her eyes. "We really have two objectives here. We have to find the mole and we have to find the Dangerous Double," she said, ticking off the items on her fingers. "Like you said, we don't have much time. The best way is to split the cases. You and I will have to dig through the files, interview staff—the kids can't do those things."

Albert Black seemed to chew on that. Then he nodded, slapped his knees, and got up. "That settles it. Stark: You and I will flush out the rat. And Ben and Linc here will find George Washington's coat."

"Wait—Ben and I have to work together?" I asked, jumping up.

Black grinned. "Think of it as an opportunity to bond. Oh, and there's a Presidential Medal of Freedom in it for everyone on the team—if the mission is a success."

A medal? That was even better than some certificate. Mom and Dad would love it. Still. "I'm not working with him," I said.

Ben didn't seem too excited about partnering either. "Baker here is not trained for this mission, sir. He never even went to junior agent boot camp!"

"Thank goodness," I said. "Who wants that?" Believe it or not, there's an actual boot camp for kids that all the agencies use. It churns out junior agents like Ben on a regular basis.

Ben gave me a death-ray look. "You need training to be an effective agent—not that you'd know anything about that." He turned his attention back to Albert Black. "Baker simply cannot handle the pressures of secret agent life. With all due respect—"

Albert Black put his hand on Ben's shoulder and pushed down. "Make it work, Agent Green. *With all due respect.*"

Ben clenched his jaw. "Yessir," he mumbled.

"The ball is on Thursday evening at seven. You kids have just . . ." Black checked his watch. "Fifty-five hours to get this coat."

Fifty-five hours. I could almost hear the clock ticking inside my head.

No pressure, right?

TUESDAY, NOON

55 HOURS UNTIL THE BALL

"NOBODY HAS A CLUE WHERE THE DAN-
gerous Double is, so time's a-wastin'." Black pointed his finger
at me, like he just remembered something. "Oh, you'll like
this: I called in some help for you both. I figured you could
use a gadget or two."

I grinned from ear to ear. "You brought Henry?"

Henry's this scrawny kid with red hair, freckles, and
glasses—and he's a total genius. For my last mission, he gave
me a parachute and a device called the Double Detector that
helped me find the evil *Mona Lisa*. But Henry isn't just super-
smart. He's also a great friend.

"Permission to speak freely, sir?" Ben asked Albert Black.

Black nodded.

"I do not require the issue of any *gadgets*. Sir." Ben pulled the junior agent training manual from his cargo pants pocket. "The manual is all the help I need."

Black shrugged. "Suit yourself." He looked at me, then at Ben. "I don't care how you get it done, but you bring me that Dangerous Double *before* Thursday seven o'clock. Get it?"

"Got it," I said.

"Affirmative," Ben said.

Stark gave us all a piece of paper with everyone's phone number to program into our phones. Then Black and Stark huddled at the other side of the room, going over their plans to flush out the mole or whatever.

Finally, it was just Ben and me. And I wanted to clock the guy but knew I had to take the high road, like Mom always tells me to do when I get into it with someone at school.

Ben had his arms crossed and pretty much looked like I felt. Fuming mad.

"Well, I'm going to see Henry and get some gear," I said. "But you're too good for that."

Ben squinted. "All I need is my training. A real secret agent doesn't require a *Double Determinator*, or whatever your little friend came up with."

"For your information, it's called a Double *Detector*. And it saved our mission the last time, if you remember." I pointed at his cargo pocket, where I knew he stuck his little book. "So you think that manual there will help you find George Washington's coat?"

"Affirmative."

"*Affirmative?* What are you—a robot?" We'd only been around each other for a couple of hours and I was already sick of the guy. "Nobody uses words like that, you know."

"You just don't like that I'm a real secret agent."

"*Junior* secret agent." So much for taking the high road. I forced myself to step back.

He squinted again. "This is impossible. They teamed me up with an amateur." He glanced over my shoulder, looking for a way out. Like he was waiting for Black or Stark to tell him I was off the case so he could be the superhero.

"You think you're better than me," I said. My blood was pumping through my veins like hot motor oil.

He looked at me with fire in his eyes. "Yes, I do. While you were riding your skateboard in Cowpoke, California, I was undercover in Cameroon, hunting down a—never mind, that is top secret."

"It's Lompoc, for your information. No cows there."

"This is not going to work," Ben said. He straightened and puffed out his chest to declare, "I cannot work with a civilian."

"Well, we agree there." I give him an icy smile. "I can't work with you either." Let's face it: I'd probably make the guy eat his junior agent training manual or something. "And you're wrong, you know. I *can* do this, and I'll be better at it than you."

Ben took a step forward and another. Until our noses were just inches apart. "Is that a challenge?"

"Absolutely." And I had a brilliant idea. A way for us to go our separate ways but still get the mission done. "Let's make it a bet. Whoever brings the Dangerous Double back here first wins."

Ben stepped back and laughed at that. "Fine."

"And that person gets to claim the title of best junior secret agent ever."

Ben clenched his teeth. "Let's up the ante. If I win—no, *when* I win, you'll give me your Presidential Medal of Freedom. You'll walk away empty-handed."

That made me pause. I really wanted that medal—Mom and Dad would be so proud. But I was confident I could beat Ben.

"Are you in, Baker?"

I nodded. "Game on, *Agent* Green."

TUESDAY, 12:15 P.M.

BEN AND I PUSHED THROUGH THE CON-
ference room doorway at the same time. I watched him get
on the elevator before I went back to ask Stark where I could
find Henry. Turns out he was just down the hall in room 418.

I took a deep breath as I made my way over there. Why
did I let Ben get under my skin like that?

Henry lit up when I knocked on the open door.

I instantly felt better. "Hey, Henry."

"Linc!" Henry called from behind the desk. There was a
table between us, with a cardboard box and a tool kit on it.
"Come in."

I wasn't sure how you were supposed to greet your gadget
guy who is also your friend, so I gave him a knuckle punch.

Henry gave me a big grin. "Isn't this great? The team is back together again." He rubbed his hands. "And I cooked up some good stuff for you and Ben."

I shook my head. "No dice on the gadgets for Ben. He has his junior secret agent manual to beat the bad guys over the head with." I told Henry about our little run-in.

"Jeez, who messed with his cereal this morning, huh?" Henry knew what a pain Ben could be. They were at junior agent boot camp together and didn't exactly get along. "But what if he wins? You'd lose out on the medal."

"With your gadgets, I'll come out on top," I said, hoping I sounded confident. "I can't wait to see what you've cooked up for me. Did Albert Black tell you about the case?"

"George Washington's coat? Yeah, it's a real toughie." Henry leaned on the box, looking lost in thought. "So where are you going to start?"

"I was hoping you might have something to go on. I didn't pay attention much when I learned about Washington in school." The truth was that I barely paid attention at all. I usually fell into a mental coma when someone started saying "in 1776, blah blah."

"I can't say I remember much myself. He had fake teeth and was a big-time hero during the Revolutionary War." Henry stared at the ceiling, like the historical clues were written on the ceiling tiles. "He could have been a king, you know. But he didn't want that kind of power. Washington was one of those real straight arrows."

"Straight arrow—that's all you got?" I groaned. "How am

I going to find the Dangerous Double?"

"Sorry." Henry was cutting the box open. "I'm the tech guy, not a historian. You know, you might want to try the Library of Congress. Just about anything you can think of is archived there. You never know what could help."

"Yeah," I said, trying to hide my disappointment. Digging through archives didn't exactly sound like fun.

"Maybe these gadgets will cheer you up." Henry reached inside the box and pulled out two black plastic balls with holes in them. He handed one to me.

It was about the size of a Ping-Pong ball but felt heavier. "What does it do?" I pushed a tiny red button, and all of a sudden, there was the loudest blaring noise. Police sirens, loud enough to make you deaf for a few hours. "Help!"

Henry snatched it from my hands and pushed the red button again. The noise stopped. "I call it 'Ruckus on a Roll.' I used my baby brother's little toy police cars to make it. Loud, huh?"

"What?"

"I said that it was loud. Wait—you're messing with me." Henry smiled. "That was good."

"A police siren might make a bad dude take a hike." After this mission was over, I might just try to snatch one to bring back home. The Ruckus on a Roll could come in handy during a test or something.

"Since Ben's not interested, you can have two," Henry said, reminding me of the mission. He handed me the balls. "The button is recessed, so the Ruckus won't go off in your bag."

I put the two balls in my backpack.

Next, Henry took some gum from his pocket and put it in his mouth. While chewing, he unpacked two rectangular strips of plastic. They looked like mousetraps. Henry placed one on his palm. "You're gonna love it." Then he took the wad of wet gum from his mouth.

"Gross, Henry!"

He shrugged. "You can't be picky when it comes to science." He stuck the gob on the small square plate. Then he held his hand out, like he was Spider-Man ready to toss a web from his wrist. Then he used his right index finger to push a small button and—

Splat! Almost instantly, the gum was pasted against the far wall.

"This is the coolest slingshot ever, Henry!"

"I call it the Sure Shot. Just be careful what you put on it. Nothing hard or you'll shoot someone's eye out."

"Soft objects only, got it." I put the two Sure Shots in my backpack.

"Oh, and last but not least." Henry reached into the box and pulled out some folded-up plastic thing. It was about the size of a rolled beach towel.

"It's a boat," I said.

"Pretty much. But I made it ultra-light and compact, out of this new material I invented. I had one for you and one for Ben, but I'll keep his for me." Henry pointed to a red plastic ring. "You pull this to inflate it."

I didn't think I'd be boating on this mission but put it inside the bottom pocket of my backpack that I normally use for my gym shoes. The boat would just smell like stinky socks if I wound up using it.

"Well, thanks, Henry. You know I couldn't do this without you. Ben doesn't know what he's missing."

Henry waved the compliment away, but I could tell he was proud of himself. He should be—the guy is the smartest twelve-year-old I know.

"Hey, you want to come with me to the Library of Congress?" I really wanted some company, and Henry was more of a book guy than me.

Henry shook his head. "Stark called me just before you got here. She wants me working on some data analysis. We're looking for the mole, and I think I have a program that might be able to help."

Henry went on for a while about how he was going to work his high-tech magic to find the mole, but it all got a little too complicated for me. I zipped up my backpack and nodded every once in a while, pretending to understand what he was talking about.

"So you're going to do some research?" Henry asked.

"Yeah, I guess I better get started." I said bye to my friend. Those Library of Congress archives were probably a lot like Pandora files. Fun, right?

I took the elevator down. When the doors opened and I got off, I turned left down a hall. And I almost ran down a girl with red shoulder-length hair.

"Hey," she said, like I was supposed to know who she was. Honestly, I had no idea.

But then I remembered the files I read on the plane, the ones on the president and her family. The photos of the first daughter.

It took me a second, but then I recognized the twinkle in her eye. "Amy?"

10

TUESDAY, 1 P.M.

54 HOURS UNTIL THE BALL

I GLANCED AROUND, BUT NO ONE IN THE hall seemed to notice us. "Where's your Secret Service person?" This was the first daughter I was talking to, after all. There had to be some security.

"You mean babysitter?" Amy pulled me along inside the visitor center. "Steve's over there." She pointed across the room. The place was huge, with high ceilings, white stone archways, and red carpet—it looked like a mini-version of the White House. Amy's Secret Service guy Steve stood near a giant black-and-white historical poster of the White House. He looked our way and smiled.

"He seems nice."

Amy nodded. "Steve lets me go where I want, as long as I let him come along." She pulled at her fake red hair. "And I have to wear this wig."

"It does make you hard to recognize," I said.

"Sometimes, he makes me wear these glasses and this hat." She pulled a black knit cap from her pocket and a pair of red plastic-rimmed glasses.

"Yikes."

"No kidding." She stuffed the hat and glasses back in her pocket. "I'm glad I found you. Steve saw Wilson come get you guys. I guessed you were going to the clubhouse meeting with Mom and figured you'd eventually come out here."

I leaned closer and whispered, "You've been down to the clubhouse?" The visitor center was pretty busy, but the place was so huge that it was easy to stay out of earshot.

"Only once, during the first week after we moved here." Amy sounded sad. "After that, Mom kind of made everything top secret."

Top secret—that reminded me of my hunt for the coat and how Ben was already way ahead of me. "Listen, I'd love to hang around here and talk, but I have a mission."

"Can I come?"

I glanced at Steve. He was smiling at some pretty blond lady walking by. She gave him the stink eye. "Is he going to be okay with that?"

"Steve's easy. He goes where I go." Amy smiled. "So where *are* we going?"

I should have told her not to come, but then, I could really use some help finding my way around DC. "The Library of Congress," I said as we walked toward the visitor center exit. I could feel Steve hanging behind us, like a piece of gum stuck to my shoe.

Outside, Amy pointed past the blue awnings of the visitor center and behind the Herbert C. Hoover Building. "That's this way."

I trailed, too busy gawking at the White House to my left.

But then Amy pulled me by the coat sleeve. "Let's go," she said.

We started walking, and I buttoned my coat. "Why are we going to the Library of Congress, exactly?" Amy asked.

"I'm looking for this . . . artifact." We'd left the White House and the visitor center behind us now. We were walking past more imposing buildings to the right and some kind of fancy lawn to our left.

Amy leaned close and waited for a group of people to pass before whispering, "Is it a Dangerous Double you're finding for Pandora?"

I glanced behind me, but Steve was far enough back. He wouldn't hear our conversation. "How do you know about all that?"

"I borrowed the files from Mom." Amy shrugged like it was no big deal. "You're Linc Baker, but you're here as Ben, right?"

I nodded.

"That's what Steve thinks, so your cover is still good. Anyway, it was all there—your first case in Paris and everything.

You sure get arrested a lot," she added with a snicker.

"You stole the Pandora files?"

"*Borrowed,*" Amy corrected. We stopped at a crosswalk.

"Then you know about the threat to your family and everything?"

Amy nodded. "Steve showed me the email and told me there was an increased security risk. That Dagger person wants to kill us." The light turned green, and we crossed the street.

"Aren't you scared?" I whispered. Not that anyone around us paid any attention. People were just passing like there was no big threat to the White House.

"I'm not afraid," Amy said. She had to be lying, but I figured maybe now was not the time to call her on it.

So we walked along Pennsylvania Avenue, which was huge and wide, with three lanes of traffic going in either direction. I told her about the George Washington coat and the bet I had with Ben to find the coat first. "Apparently the Library of Congress has some George Washington archives."

Amy laughed. "Oh yeah, *some* is the word. Like, *sixty-five thousand* documents."

I stopped and coughed. "Seriously?"

"You bet. There are diaries, letters, military documents—you name it, the Library of Congress has it archived. I borrowed a few documents once," Amy mused.

Of course she did.

"Not a good idea." Her face was very serious now.

I groaned. "I don't have time to dig through tens of thousands of files."

"I know where to go." Amy pulled my arm. "Come on." Steve scrambled to keep up with her brisk pace.

"Where are we going?"

"To the International Spy Museum."

11

AMY GAVE ME A SMILE. "YOU KNOW,
George Washington was a spy."

I tried to picture the guy on my dollar bill in black clothes and sunglasses. George Washington, super-spy. I laughed. "No way."

"Oh yes." Amy nodded. "Did you know Revolutionary War spies used invisible ink to send messages between the lines of documents?"

I didn't. That spy history stuff sounded like the secret club Sam, Daryl, and I had in second grade. Only this was serious business.

As we kept walking, Amy told me about all the ways spies used to send messages. She was explaining something about laundry hanging to dry and that being a code, but I was too busy trying not to gawk at all the imposing buildings we passed to pay much attention. Washington, DC, was like a big fat history lesson, only we were walking in it.

We took a left on 9th and then a right on F Street, where the buildings were closer together.

"Come on," Amy said. "This is it." She pointed to a large brick building with red awnings and a giant movie-theater-style billboard across the front.

INTERNATIONAL SPY MUSEUM

"They really don't want you to miss it, huh?" I followed Amy into the museum lobby and to the ticket booth.

"Is Andrea here?" Amy asked the lady behind the counter. The lady nodded and picked up the phone to call her.

"I'm a member here. You can be my guest," Amy said to me. She bounced on her heels, and I saw that both her shoes were untied.

"Your laces." I didn't want her taking a dive if we had to make a run for it.

Amy sighed and knelt down to fix them while Steve found a spot to sit on a bench near the gift shop to the left of the lobby. The store had a retro vibe with the old spy photos and books—Grandpa would love it.

"Well, look who's here," I heard behind me. A woman with super-short black hair in a black suit and a red shirt walked up to meet us. "Amy," she said.

"Hey, Andrea."

They hugged, then Andrea looked at Amy, holding her by the shoulders. "Wait—shouldn't you be in school right now?"

"I have the afternoon off. So relax," Amy said, pulling away from her grip.

"If you're sure," Andrea said with a frown. "The last time I had you here during school hours, I ended up being called in by your mother. And I don't like to get on the US president's bad side. If you're cutting school—"

"I'm not." She pointed to Steve on the bench, who was studying a museum brochure. "See, I have my babysitter along and everything." Amy poked me with her elbow. "Introduce yourself."

"Benjamin Green," I said, remembering my cover. I shook the woman's hand. "I'm supposed to be in school, but the CIA gave me a note."

That got me a laugh from Andrea. "Let's walk." We followed her past the booth down a narrow hall. We went left, and I immediately felt like I was in a time warp. There was an old car and a phone booth to our left and a café exhibit to our right. "That's the Berlin Café," Andrea said when she saw me looking around. "This part of the museum covers the Cold War—but I don't think you came here for a tour, did you?"

"You're right. We need your help. Well, my friend Ben does," Amy said.

"I'm looking for something that used to belong to George Washington," I said. This top secret business was really annoying sometimes. I didn't know how much I should tell her.

"The first American spy," Andrea said with a smile to Amy. "You came to the right place. I've done a lot of research on his spy operation."

"Washington's organization was called the Culper Ring," Amy said. "Its members would collect information on British movements and then pass it to the right people. The intelligence gathered by the Culper Ring spies kept the British from taking West Point during the Revolutionary War and took down Benedict Arnold—right, Andrea?"

Andrea nodded. "Let's find a quiet spot," she said, eyeing a tour group that came in behind us. She led us down a tunnel that looked a little like the White House passage to the clubhouse, only smaller. There were planks on the floor and sandbags stacked against the walls.

"So who were these Culper Ring spies anyway?" I asked.

"The man who ran the operation was Benjamin Tallmadge," Andrea said. The dim light in the tunnel cast shadows across her face. "He recruited ordinary citizens to deliver messages. We've identified almost all the members. And then there was George Washington, of course. He ordered the Culper Ring into existence. But the members of the ring didn't know each other's names—they all had numbers instead."

"To keep them safe, right?" Amy asked. You could tell she was really into all that spy stuff.

"Tallmadge kept a code dictionary to send messages," Andrea said. "It also identified the members of the ring. George Washington was code-named Seven-Eleven."

I remembered from my meeting with the president that Tallmadge helped Washington hide the Dangerous Double. "So they were friends."

Andrea nodded.

"If Washington had to hide something, a dangerous secret," Amy said, glancing at me, "would he use the Culper Ring?"

Andrea thought about that for a moment. "Yes, without a doubt." She hesitated and then motioned for us to move closer. There was an older couple moving past us in the tunnel, but they didn't seem to care what we were up to.

"Only one member of the Culper Ring remained unidentified," Andrea continued. "This spy was known only as Three-Five-Five. The book called her simply 'Lady.' It's thought that Agent Three-Five-Five held something important of Washington's. Something he needed to keep from the public."

"But that was a couple hundred years ago. So who has this, um, secret *now*?" I asked Andrea. Two museum visitors came into the tunnel, so we moved back to the Berlin Café.

"No one knows," Andrea said. "There's been talk that the Culper Ring didn't dissolve after the Revolutionary War. That with the unidentified Agent Three-Five-Five, the spy ring continued down the generations."

"That's it," I said. "We need to find this new Culper Ring."

12

TUESDAY, 2:30 P.M.

"IT'S JUST CIA FOLKLORE," ANDREA ADDED,
straightening a little. "But if I was looking for a secret George
Washington hid, I would look for the Culper Ring."

"And where would we look?" I asked.

"Deep, *deep* undercover," Andrea whispered, like that
was the only logical answer.

I was getting antsy and practically shouted, "There are
lives on the line here. Amy's, for one. We need to contact this
Culper Ring now!"

Andrea could tell I wasn't kidding, and she said, "Okay.
I wouldn't give you this if it wasn't for Amy. And President
Griffin." She opened her wallet and pulled out a dollar bill.

I took the dollar and then saw that it was cut in

half—deliberately, from the looks of it, and in a zigzag pattern. "What's this?"

"It's an old spy trick." Amy pulled the bill from my hand and held it up.

Quickly glancing around the Berlin Café exhibit, Andrea pushed Amy's arm down. "Keep that out of sight!"

"It's a way to show someone you're legit," Amy whispered to me. "We connect this part of the dollar to the other half. . . ."

"That way, my contact knows I sent you. He'll be able to get you in touch with the next link in the chain. This is deep cover we're talking about." Andrea pulled a piece of paper from her pocket and scribbled something down. "Go to this address. Order a dozen and an extra for the cat—say it *exactly* like that," she said with an urgent sound to her voice. "That's our code."

I took the paper and the cut-up dollar bill. Seeing Washington on it reminded me of the coat, and how dangerous its invincibility power could be if it fell into the wrong hands. I felt the pressure to hurry up and find the Dangerous Double.

We walked back to the museum lobby. I was a little sorry I wouldn't get to see the rest of the place—for a museum, it looked pretty cool. But I was on a mission here. No time for sightseeing.

"I hope you're ready for the world of deep-cover spies, Benjamin," Andrea said to me before walking us out. "It can drive you crazy with paranoia just to figure out who to trust."

"This isn't my first case," I said. Technically, it was only my second, but there was no need to point that out.

"Good luck," Andrea added with a little wave, and she left us near the gift shop, where Steve was napping on the bench, his chin resting on his chest.

"Should we wake him up?" I asked Amy.

She shook her head. "He'll catch up with us. Steve always tracks me by my phone's signal. Where are we going anyway?"

I opened the piece of paper.

"'Frank: 1100 Maine Ave. SW.'"

"Really?" Amy turned around and cocked her head, like she didn't believe me.

I waved the piece of paper. "What's so special about 1100 Maine Avenue?"

"It's a fish market. Also known as the Fish Wharf." Amy smiled. "I hope you're hungry."

13

THE FISH WHARF WAS ON THE POTOMAC,
the river that runs right through Washington, DC. We
walked for almost half an hour to get there—so yes, I was
ready for some food. The smell of fish was strong but in a
good, smoky way.

I glanced around the packed market. When I looked
closer, I saw that it was actually a pier. The vendors were
barges that wrapped around it. At the far end, the biggest fish
shop had a giant image of a fisherman on the roof that looked
a lot like a cartoon. There were about ten fish vendors with
clusters of people in front of each one.

"So now what?" I asked.

Amy looked at the piece of paper again. "We're looking for someone named Frank."

There was no easy way to do this. We'd have to brave the crowd. "Let's just ask at each stand, okay?"

We found one Frank and ordered a dozen and an extra for the cat—as it turns out, we were buying crabs. Frank put them in a large paper bag, like the kind you'd get your groceries in, and tossed them with a cup of seasoning. Then he steamed the food, bag and all. I paid, and that was it.

"Okay, so maybe that wasn't our Frank," Amy said as we walked away with our bag of crabs. "Frank is a common name, right? Let's try again at another stand."

We waited in line for fifteen minutes—no Frank. Then another twenty minutes at different vendors, which netted us an annoyed John, a cranky Wanda, and finally, we hit pay dirt and found another Frank. Frank Two gave us our second bag of crabs. He showed no sign of getting our coded message, so all this visit had gotten us was a fishy lunch.

"I'm too hungry to think," I said, ready for a break. "Let's just eat, and then we'll go back and try again."

We walked to the left of the Fish Warf, to an area along the Potomac with picnic tables. There was a long bar-like counter made out of two-by-four planks. The counter ran parallel to the river, and there were some people standing, eating their lunch. It was pretty scenic, I have to admit.

And I got why the people of Washington, DC, like their crabs. First, you get to whack the heck out of the shells inside your paper bag with this little hammer—perfect if you've had a long day dealing with weird spy stuff. Then you open the bag and get to eat with your hands. And the crabs are plain awesome.

"Good, huh?" Amy said as she ripped her paper bag a little more. "Best in the city, if you ask me."

I was about to tell her that there was a piece of crab hanging from her lip when a big shadow fell over us. It was Frank Two.

"An extra for the cat, huh?" Frank said, leaning on the counter. He was huge, three hundred pounds of heft at least, and at least six-four tall. The guy could take me down in a heartbeat. He sized me up, thinking pretty much the same thing. "I never expected kids."

"Why not?" Amy piped up behind me. Way to go, Amy, messing with the giant and using me as a shield. "Maybe that's exactly why we make good spies."

"Shhh!" Frank Two tossed her the evilest of glares. "You don't ever say the *s* word in this city unless you're looking to get in trouble."

"Whatever." I couldn't see Amy, but I imagined she rolled her eyes.

Frank Two glanced around. "Did you bring the president?"

"Why would we do that?" Amy said. "She's got stuff to do, you know."

"He's not talking about *that* president." I dug into my pocket and pulled out my half of the dollar bill. "He's talking about *this* one." I placed the bill on the counter so it was hidden by a pile of crab legs.

Frank Two exhaled and pulled another half from his

wallet. He put it next to my half, until you couldn't tell where the zigzag split was.

"This is all really exciting," I said, careful to keep my voice down, "but how will it help us find what we're looking for?"

Frank laughed, rough and burly, like a guy who's been smoking three packs of cigarettes a day his whole life. "I know who sent you, that's how. This was just a test. I'm step one. Just the beginning, you hear me?"

"So can you tell us where we can find members of the Culper Ring?" I whispered, careful not to use the *s* word.

Frank Two pulled a pen from his breast pocket. Then he leaned over and grabbed a folded newspaper someone had left behind. "You call the classified section of the *Washington Herald*. You place an ad and make sure it's worded *exactly* like this." He scribbled something on my brown bag, ripped it off, and folded it before I could see what it was. He tucked it in my coat pocket. Thanks to Frank, I would smell like fish for days.

"Then what?" I asked.

"You wait for a message to come."

"How?" Amy asked.

Frank got all irritated. "You'll know it when it comes, okay?" He leaned close and added in a ticked-off whisper, "Did you think you would just buy some crabs and find a deep-cover spy ring?"

I kind of did, but I figured keeping my mouth shut was the best move around Frank Two.

He shook his head. "You're a disaster. Exposing me, right in my own yard."

"What do you mean?" I asked, glancing around.

Frank Two dug his fingers into my left arm. "Don't. *Look.*"

"Did someone follow us? No way."

Frank Two laughed again and kept going until it turned into a cough fest. "You're not from here, are you? Let me guess—California." He glanced at me. "Somewhere away from the city, but not too remote. Near the beach, but not with your toes in the sand. Central coast, I bet."

"I'm from Lompoc," I said, realizing too late I'd let my Ben cover slip. This guy was like a mind reader or something. "How did you know?"

"Let's just say reading people used to be my job." Frank Two stared out onto the Potomac, then up to the bridge. "You're in Washington, DC, now, kids. Home of the CIA, NSA, Secret Service—you name anything that involves secrets, it starts and ends here. This city is full of spies, wannabes, and used-to-bes."

I felt like there were crabs walking up my spine, and I couldn't move. "They're here?"

"Oh yeah." Frank Two sniffed. "That mom, pushing the baby stroller? There's no baby in there. She's CIA. Deep cover, probably. Those German tourists are new agents on the job—just look at the stupid getups."

"But we're with the CIA," I said.

"You sure about that?" Frank Two gave me a knowing smile. "Because they're tailing you like you're the enemy."

"Maybe it's because we're deep undercover and all."

"How many are here, right now?" Amy asked, glancing around.

"Six. Seven if you count Wanda over there, but she's

retired, like me." Frank Two gave Amy a grin. It looked sort of creepy, if you want to know the truth. I was wondering if he had eyes in the back of his head. Maybe those were standard issue for secret agents, like they are for moms.

"How's that even possible? I didn't see anyone follow me," I said. I may not be a Ben Green, but I was pretty sure I could spot a tail by now.

"It's their job to go unnoticed by civilians. You'll need some distraction if you want to get out of here, kids," Frank Two said.

I thought *Ruckus on a Roll* right away. But these were government agents, not all-out bad dudes—they probably wouldn't run if I set off the fake police siren.

But then I had an idea. A tried-and-true distraction that went back to the beginning of time—and it would be even better with Henry's invention. My idea wouldn't be pretty and might even get me arrested, but it could work.

I opened my backpack and handed Amy a Sure Shot. "Can you follow my lead?"

Amy nodded.

I dug my hand inside the paper bag of gooey, fishy mess, and I stuck a piece of crab on the Sure Shot.

I aimed. Took a breath.

And started slinging seafood.

14

TUESDAY, 3:57 P.M.

I SHOT MY LEFTOVERS AT THE GERMAN
tourists first (they were easy to spot with their fake mustaches
and I ♥ DC shirts), but then just shot crab parts at everyone.
Initially, there was shock, irritation, and yelling—stage one of
a food fight. You'll know this if you've ever been in one.

But once Amy joined in, it got crazy. Stage two exploded
like a bomb. Kids began tossing food around, laughing. Let's
face it: It's hard to pass up a food fight—and this was a good
one. Vendors got upset; people were yelling and shoving. It
was a big hot mess.

Distraction aplenty.

Not that Amy and I stuck around too long. We bolted,
with me following Amy as she navigated the streets of

DC. After about fifteen minutes or so of sprinting, cutting through traffic, taking shortcuts through alleyways, she finally slowed down.

"Wow, who would have thought a food fight could outwit a bunch of government agents, huh?" Amy laughed, her cheeks red from the cold wind and our sprint across the city.

"Food fights are a powerful weapon. Not to be used unless absolutely necessary," I joked, relieved that Amy was safe.

"So now what?" she asked, once we were sure no one had followed us.

I took the folded piece of brown paper from my pocket. "Now we see what the ad in the paper is about." I unfolded the paper.

Wanted ASAP: 1980 Ford pickup.

"That's it?" Amy frowned.

"How is the Culper Ring supposed to know how to contact me?" I mumbled. This made no sense at all.

"Maybe they have their ways of finding you." Amy shrugged. "Nothing surprises me much after living around Secret Service agents. These spy types know everything."

"I hope you're right." I tucked the paper back in my pocket. "Maybe I'll put in Ben's name and my motel room, just in case."

"I haven't had this much fun since I moved here." Amy practically bounced when she walked. "It's been pretty hard to make friends, being the first daughter."

"I can't even imagine." I'd lived in Lompoc all my life, same house, same friends. "So what do you do for fun, besides borrowing things?"

She smiled. "I get out and see the city whenever I can."

We were getting close to the International Spy Museum now, and I saw a guy in a suit running our way, waving both his arms.

"Steve?" Amy stopped.

Steve looked all sweaty and confused as he slowed his pace. "Where did you go?" he asked Amy, leaning on his knees to catch his breath. "I only nodded off for a second—I had a late night. When I woke up, Andrea said you'd left."

Amy gave him her best I'm-so-sorry smile. "You looked so peaceful, and I know how hard you work. I didn't want to wake you."

"We went to catch some lunch," I added.

"And we threw it, too," Amy joked. Then she remembered she was supposed to be serious. "I'm so, *so* sorry, Steve."

Steve still looked confused, but her apology seemed to have mellowed him out. "We need to get you back home now. This isn't safe. If your mother and my boss hear you were out of my sight, they'll kill me."

Amy looped her arm in Steve's. "I won't tell them if you won't."

Steve gave her a relieved smile. "But we need to hurry back now."

We made our way back to the motel. Amy waved goodbye to me, and she and Steve took off to get his car.

Me, I had a strange feeling in my gut, and it wasn't the crab talking. I felt guilty. Even though Amy was great help, I knew that her coming with me on the mission was a very bad idea. Dagger was out to kill the president and her family—that included first daughter Amy. As much fun as it was to have a friend and sidekick out here, I put Amy in danger.

I had to do this on my own.

By the time I made it up to my room, the adrenaline from our crabby food fight had worn off. I was hungry, tired, cold, and reeked of fish.

I called and placed the ad in the paper. The guy who took my message didn't seem at all surprised I was in search of a Ford pickup. It took only a few minutes, and when I hung up, it was just me and my silent room.

And I wasn't so confident about beating Benjamin Green anymore. What if this was a dead end? It was after five o'clock, which meant I had less than fifty hours until the ball—what if Frank's lead was a total dud? What if the new Culper Ring was just a legend?

Even a hot shower and a little cartoon watching didn't make me feel any better. So I did what every twelve-year-old secret agent double does when the chips are down.

I called home.

The phone rang about half-a-dozen times. I did some quick math, and I calculated that since it was six o'clock in DC, it was three in the afternoon in California. But no one answered. So I left a message, telling everyone I was fine and that I'd try to call again tomorrow. I hung up, feeling kind of down.

Then my phone rang, startling me from this feeling-sorry-for-myself moment. I checked my little caller ID screen.

Unknown Caller. Could it be my next lead? But the newspaper wouldn't be out until morning.

I answered anyway. "Yes?"

"Agent Green."

"Um, affirmative," I said, deciding it was probably safest just to play along.

"This is Hans. I have your package."

15

BENJAMIN GREEN WAS GETTING A PACK-
age. Actually, *I* was the one getting a package. This was great!

"Okay. I mean, that's good."

"Pick it up at 14th and G. Be here by nine thirty." And this Hans guy hung up.

My heart was racing as I reached for a notepad to write the information down. I'd just gotten a freebie lead. This was awesome!

I smiled as I folded the piece of paper. Who knew, maybe Ben really had beaten me—maybe the coat was in the package! I could swoop in and steal the victory right from under his nose.

Then I jumped as my phone rang again. *Unknown Caller.*

What if Hans figured out he wasn't calling Ben but really me?

I hesitated for a second. But answered anyway. "Hello?"

"Linc! It's Amy." She sounded so excited.

"Amy. How did you even get this number?"

"Jeez, nice to talk to you, too. Earlier today, I took your phone and looked."

"You stole my phone?"

"*Bor-rowed.* And only long enough to get your number," she went on, like swiping a friend's phone was no big deal. "Did you wash the crab stink off?" she asked.

"Sort of." Not really, to tell you the truth.

"You wanna come for dinner?"

"At the White House?"

Amy laughed. "Yeah. We do eat here, you know. And it's Tuesday," she said, like that explained everything.

"What happens on Tuesday?"

"You'll see. Will you come?"

Since I'm always up for a free meal, I agreed. "Dinner at the White House. Sounds awesome." But then I remembered Ben's package. Nine thirty—I should be done with dinner by then, no sweat.

"I'll have them send a car to pick you up," Amy said.

After I put on my least wrinkly shirt, I hurried down to the lobby, not paying much attention to anything.

But I do remember feeling those goose bumps, the kind you get when someone's watching you. And I saw a cleaning lady wearing a hairnet, getting on the elevator just as I got off. I should have looked closer. Looked at her face. Spotted the loose strand of brown hair. I might've made the connection.

But I saw the big black SUV out front waiting for me. So I buttoned up my coat and forgot about that tiny alarm bell going off inside my head.

I mean, I was having dinner at the White House. Who had time to be paranoid?

16

TUESDAY, 6:45 P.M.

STEVE PICKED ME UP, WHICH WAS PRETTY
awkward. For most of the drive, he kept rambling on about
how hard it was to be on Amy's detail.

"She keeps disappearing, and then when I find her, she
acts like it was *my* fault."

"Uh-huh."

"If Amy tells the story her way to her mom, I'm out of a
job." He continued talking, but I tuned him out after a few
minutes. I couldn't stop thinking about what was inside Ben's
box. What if it was the coat? Or maybe it was a piece of the
puzzle I could use to beat him to the coat. I could almost
imagine holding the Dangerous Double and handing it to
the president. She would thank me, and maybe I'd get that

Presidential Medal of Freedom. . . .

"Ben! We're here," Steve said, stirring me from my thoughts. He'd pulled up at the north end of the White House, under the portico I'd seen from the West Wing that morning.

"I guess I get the royal treatment for dinner, huh?" I joked, but Steve just gave me a blank stare. The guy had no sense of humor.

Amy was waiting by the door when I got out. No red wig this time—just her own mop of blond curls, which looked much better on her. "Thanks for coming!" she said over her shoulder. I followed her inside as Steve went to park the car. "You're lucky that it's Tuesday."

"Why's that?"

"Taco Tuesday, of course!" Amy acted like I was so dumb for not getting that.

"I know about Taco Tuesday. I just didn't picture your family, you know, eating normal food." This was the president we're talking about, come on. Tacos were more for the Baker family.

"This is the Entrance Hall," Amy said with pride. "We're on the state floor now." We were in a big reception hall, with tall ceilings, a fancy glass chandelier, and white-and-tan-checked marble floors. I felt totally out of place in my jeans and sneakers but tried not to show it.

"Cool, huh?" Amy said next to me. "This is the official entrance for visitors. We have a few minutes before dinner. Come on, I'll show you where the ball is going to be."

I followed her between these white columns, and we took a left.

"This is the Cross Hall. And over there are the Red, Blue, and Green Rooms." Amy waved to the right as we walked. When the hall ended at a doorway, Amy said, "This is the East Room."

It was roped off, so we had to look from the doorway. I saw tall ceilings, fancy cream curtains, and several sparkly chandeliers hanging from the ceiling. A grand piano sat near the back wall. There were five guys in black pants and white shirts, setting up tables and unrolling a giant rug.

"This is where the costume ball will be?" I asked.

Amy nodded. "If there's a party at the White House, it's usually held in here. You know, when we first moved in, Wilson told me that Theodore Roosevelt's kids roller-skated in here," she added.

I looked at the zigzagged wooden floor and how big the room was. "It would be awesome to skateboard in here."

"The staff would have a cow if you did that," Amy said with a grin.

George Washington gave me a stern look from an oil painting on the wall, reminding me of the mission.

Amy looked at her watch. "Dinner's at seven, so we should head to the kitchen."

"Okay." Then I remembered my Ben package pickup later that night. "I just have to leave at nine."

"Why?"

"Sleep," I lied. "I need to rest up for tomorrow."

"That's right—we're on a mission," Amy whispered so Steve wouldn't hear us. We turned away from the East Room and then took a right up a stairway.

"Doesn't Steve come along?" I asked as we made our way up the stairs.

Amy shook her head. "Nope. Family quarters upstairs. It's the one place Secret Service leaves us alone."

We went upstairs, down a hall to the left, and into the kitchen. It looked pretty standard with white cabinets, but nice—not like the Baker kitchen, but more like my friend Sam's. Then I spotted Ben. He was already sitting at the table.

I turned around and faced Amy. "You invited *him*?"

Amy shrugged. "Mom said I should."

"That's okay," I lied.

"He came in through the West Wing so we wouldn't blow your cover," Amy added.

I faced Ben and forced a smile as I sat across from him at the kitchen table. "How's the mission coming along?"

"Good." He clenched his jaw. "I'm making great progress."

"Using your manual."

"That's correct. How about you, Baker?" Ben asked. "Are you having fun riding your little skateboard around?"

"We're doing fine," Amy said.

I kicked her under the table. "What Amy means is *Linc* is doing fine. I have a lead already. Two leads, actually," I said, thinking of Ben's package. "How about you?"

"I have a mission plan," Ben said. "A good agent needs only one lead." Like a package.

Isn't he just full of it? The good news was that I was about to steal his one lead right from under him. "Well, nobody can be as good as you, Ben," I said.

"Maybe we shouldn't talk about the mission," Amy mumbled.

"Apologies." Ben took his knife and fork.

"I'm sorry, too." I guess we were being kind of rude, what with us being dinner guests and all.

"This looks delicious," Ben said as he took a plate of tacos from the chef.

"I hope you weren't expecting something fancy," Amy said. "For Taco Tuesday, I like to eat in the kitchen with Mom. That way it feels more like normal, you know?"

"We have dinner in front of the TV a lot," I said as I took my plate. The mini-tacos were arranged in a perfect star pattern, like each one was a point. "My mom's a nurse, and she's going to school, too. Most of the time it's just me, Dad, and Grandpa."

"My parents are usually working late," Ben said. He was trying to cut his taco but only managed to make a big pile of crumbs, meat, and salsa.

Amy laughed as she picked up a taco. "You should eat with your hands."

Ben blushed but then took her lead. I guess they don't teach tacos at the junior agent boot camp.

"Shouldn't we wait for your mom?" I asked Amy.

She shook her head. "No. She's coming, though. . . ." Her voice trailed. "Just a little later than expected."

I still felt weird about messing up that perfect plate. But once Amy started eating, making a mess and all, I dug in, too.

"These are the best tacos ever." They really were, no lie. If you ever get to visit the White House, I highly suggest you order the taco plate.

I was about to ask if I could have more when President Griffin walked in. Now, that will make you choke on your dinner, let me tell you.

Ben jumped up, like he was at attention or something.

"I'm so sorry I'm late." President Griffin kissed Amy on the head. "This presidential ball . . . Never mind. I wasn't going to miss out on Taco Tuesday."

"I can see why," I said. "I'm ready for seconds."

"Good. And you can sit down, Benjamin."

Ben sat back down, looking a little lost. "Ma'am."

President Griffin pulled up a chair, and the chef brought her a plate like ours along with a glass of water. "You can call me by my first name, guys. I'm Dorothy." She rolled up the sleeves of her crisp white blouse. "I'm off duty for the next half hour."

Amy looked really happy with that.

"I love Taco Tuesday." President Griffin (I couldn't call her Dorothy, come on now) took her first bite of taco and closed her eyes as she chewed.

Ben and I got seconds while Amy and her mom argued over the latest episode of some show I didn't watch. It was like our dinner table, only we were at the White House. It was weird. Ben and I mostly listened.

By eight o'clock, President Griffin folded her napkin and placed it on her empty plate. "I have a few more briefs to go over," she said with a sigh.

"Yeah, of course." Amy tried to hide her disappointment, but no one was buying it. "Thanks for coming, Mom."

"Wouldn't miss it."

"You guys should have a Waffle Wednesday," I joked, trying to cheer Amy up. Ben frowned—that guy just didn't know when a good lame joke was the perfect dessert.

"Turkey Thursday," Amy said with a smile.

"Falafel Friday," President Griffin added with a laugh, too. "You're right, Linc—we need to have dinner together every night, not just on Tuesdays."

I was about to tell them about my mom's spaghetti and meatball dinner when Wilson rushed into the kitchen. "Madam President," he said, sounding out of breath. "There's been a development."

Ben jumped up again. "The mission?" he asked.

Wilson nodded. "You kids better come with us."

"Me too?" Amy asked, practically bouncing out of her seat.

President Griffin got up and gave Amy a sad smile. "Not you, sweetheart. You need to stay safe."

I felt bad, but we had to go. I grabbed my backpack.

Amy slumped in her seat as we followed Wilson. It felt wrong, leaving her sitting at the kitchen table by herself, but I wasn't exactly in charge.

So I tried to shrug off the bad vibe as we raced through the tunnel and to the clubhouse beyond the metal door. I was nervous, clutching my dad's compass on my backpack. There was no excitement at all this time around—we knew that bad news was waiting for us.

Black and Stark greeted us and passed several copies of a printed email. It took me a second to scan the page:

TO: Mustang
FROM: Dagger
Babushka has been obtained. Artifact in sight.
Move forward with plan as scheduled.

I raised my hand like I was in class. "Um, what's a Babushka?"

Stark glanced at President Griffin, who still had her eyes glued to the paper.

Ben looked confused, too—the guy didn't know everything after all.

Stark took a breath before she said, "A Babushka is an extremely dangerous explosive device."

The bad guy had a bomb.

17

"THIS BABUSHKA IS BAD NEWS," AGENT
Stark said with a quiver in her voice. "It's a Russian-made bomb, and when it is triggered—"

"Can we just focus on a solution here?" President Griffin said, interrupting Stark. She folded the printout, and I saw that her hands were trembling. "We're talking about my daughter's safety. Do we know that this bomb threat is even valid?"

Stark nodded. "We checked the inventory, ma'am. A Babushka went missing from one of our military installations a few days ago."

President Griffin nodded, looking defeated.

"But the bad guy still doesn't have the Dangerous Double,

83

right?" I said, trying to look on the bright side. "So if we find it first, he won't be able to go forward with his plan." I was about to add "and blow up the White House," but stopped myself.

"How is the search for the coat going, kids?" Black asked.

"I'm waiting on something, but I have a plan," Ben said.

"I have a solid lead, too," I added, hoping I sounded confident. "Two leads, actually." I was counting Ben's package and the spy contact.

"How about the search for the mole?" President Griffin asked Black and Stark. "Are you any closer to uncovering the traitor's identity?"

Stark looked flustered, which I took as a bad sign. "This Dagger person used staff computers to send the emails. So far, it's proving hard to find a trail." Her voice faded

"We're working on it, Madam President," Black said. "But in light of this escalated threat, you may want to reconsider canceling the ball."

"No," President Griffin said resolutely. "Celebrating America's History has been planned for months—there are events at the Smithsonian, Mount Vernon. I'm scheduled to give a speech at the Lincoln Memorial for festivities on Friday." She handed her printout to Stark. "I won't be terrorized—and what's to say this Dagger person won't strike next week, or next month?"

We were all silent, because everyone knew she was right. We had to catch the bad guy, and that meant going ahead with the ball.

President Griffin looked at Black, then to Stark. "Find the

mole and the Dangerous Double." She looked at her watch. "You have just over forty-six hours."

Ben, President Griffin, Wilson, Stark, and I went back down the tunnel to the White House after Albert Black assured the president we were on the case.

"How's your search for the Dangerous Double coming?" Ben asked behind me as we walked. I tried hard not to seem like we were together. Stark, President Griffin, and Wilson were in deep conversation about the hunt for the mole.

"Good. Great, actually," I said, thinking of his package. "How about you? Any new clues get delivered yet?"

Ben squinted. "I'll have the artifact secured by the end of the day tomorrow, latest. I'm the top secret agent here."

"We'll see." I felt a little guilty fighting over some bet when Amy's life was on the line—even more so now that the bad guy had a bomb. Still, I couldn't wait to see what was inside the package. And I had to hurry if I was going to be on time to pick it up. "I guess we better get back to work."

We came to the basement, where Ben split off with Stark. Wilson and the president went their way.

Leaving me with some buff Secret Service guy who escorted me to my ride. I passed through the giant pillars and was on my way out through the North Portico when someone tapped me on the shoulder.

I turned around and looked at a tall guy in a dark blue suit with a little shine to it. He smiled, flashing super-white teeth.

"Um, sorry," I said.

"No need to apologize," the guy said, and he stepped back. "Actually, I was looking for you."

Uh-oh. "Really?"

"You're Benjamin Green, aren't you?"

18

TUESDAY, 9 P.M.

46 HOURS UNTIL THE BOMB

WHEN SOMEONE IN A SUIT SAYS THEY'VE been looking for you, it can only mean one thing. You're in trouble.

But I knew I was supposed to protect the whole double secret, so I rolled with the mix-up over who I was. "Yep, that's me. Benjamin Green."

"I'm Sidney Ferguson, director of National Intelligence." He dismissed the buff Secret Service dude who walked me out and motioned to the pillars behind us. "Take a walk with me."

"Sure," I said. I really had to go get the package, but Ferguson didn't look like the kind of guy who takes no for an answer. "What's up?"

"I just wanted to ask you how things were going,"

Ferguson said. He had his hands clasped behind his back as we walked back the way I came between the white pillars.

"Great," I lied.

He led me back to the Cross Hall and went right. "I hear you're Albert Black's top junior agent."

"That's right."

"How's that working for you?" Ferguson asked.

I shrugged. "Fine."

"Hmmm." Ferguson nodded, and he had a concerned look on his face. "You know, an agent's career often depends on the leadership they're under. If you want to get ahead, you need to . . . position yourself."

Huh? What was he going on about?

"I worked with Albert Black, long ago," Ferguson said. "And as you can tell, my career has progressed to director of National Intelligence." We stopped in front of the East Room. Ferguson looked inside, like he was searching for something. Then we turned back around.

I was beginning to get what this was about. Ferguson was the popular kid in school—or in this case, at the White House. "You're saying Albert Black is a loser."

Ferguson laughed. "You're a smart one, aren't you?"

"I'm Benjamin Green."

Ferguson got all serious again. "All I'm saying is that Albert Black is not who he appears to be. I would hate to see a young promising agent like you get caught in his web of lies."

We'd left the Cross Hall and were back in the North Portico. "Isn't Black on your team, CIA and all?" I asked.

Ferguson didn't answer my question. He dug into his pocket and took out a business card. "Albert Black may have used a favor to get himself inside the White House. However, he's not who he seems." Ferguson handed me his card.

"What am I supposed to do with this?"

"Call me when you find out the truth and decide to get on the right team." He stepped closer. "I wouldn't mention our talk to anyone."

"Why not?" Usually, when an adult tells you to keep a secret, it's bad news. Unless it involves a birthday present or something.

"For *your* sake, Agent Green." And Ferguson turned around and went back the way we came.

I tucked the card into my pocket. That conversation was weird, right? The stuff he said about Albert Black. *He's not who he seems.* What did that mean anyway?

I walked outside, where Steve was waiting in his black SUV. I got inside and saw the dashboard clock: It was twenty minutes after nine. "Can you step on it, Steve?"

"Sure thing." Steve raised the little window and drove me back to the Thrifty Suites in a hurry.

I couldn't relax. All I could think about was that package. Maybe the key to finding the coat was inside. I would save the president from this bomb-toting Dagger. Be the hero, and leave Ben in my dust.

I'm pretty sure I set a skateboarding speed record, the cold DC air burning my ears as I whizzed down the street. It was nine forty-five when I finally reached the address—not that it mattered. Because when I looked up, I saw the sign.

DC PACKING AND DELIVERY SERVICE

And you'll love what it said in big red letters on the glass storefront:

NOW OPEN 24 HOURS! FOR YOUR CONVENIENCE.

Thanks for mentioning the around-the-clock opening hours on the phone, Hans. I got all stressed out for nothing.

So I picked up the package from Hans, who turned out to be just some dude in a polo shirt. The box was square and had URGENT stickers all over it. It felt a little heavy.

You're dying to know what's inside, right? I was, too. But I made myself walk to the motel so I could open it in private.

While I waited for the elevator, I tried to guess what was in the box. The return address was just a place in Maryland—that told me nothing. I almost shook the box but then figured I might not want to do that. Ben was a secret agent. For all I knew, there was a weapon in there. I imagined what it might be as I rode the elevator to the fifth floor. Knives or spy equipment? Anything was possible, right?

As I got off on the fifth floor, I brushed past some bald guy in a brown leather jacket getting on the elevator. He was followed by a cleaning lady—the same woman I'd seen just before I left for dinner, with more strands of brown hair sticking out of her hairnet.

Wasn't it a little late to be cleaning rooms? And she looked vaguely familiar—I'd seen her someplace other than the motel. But my brain was too stressed for me to remember where. She gave me a smug little smile that said *I know something you don't.*

I was about to call her out when the elevator doors shut right in front of me.

I punched the elevator call button but knew it was a waste of time. The stairs! I rushed to the stairwell and dropped my board near the door. I wasn't about to leave my Ben package, but my board, I could risk coming back for.

I raced down the stairs, clutching the box, hearing my footsteps echo off the concrete walls. Fourth floor.

Third.

Second.

By the time I reached the lobby, I knew it was too late. I waited anyway, watching the elevator doors open. But it was empty.

My mystery lady and her bald friend were gone.

Then I had a gut feeling—and it wasn't just the Tuesday Tacos. I remembered where I'd seen the brown-haired woman before: on the plane that Monday. She'd swiped my file—no doubt about that now. And that same lady had been on the fifth floor. *My* floor.

Forgetting the elevator, I rushed up the stairs, two, three steps at a time, feeling the edge of the cardboard box cut into my side. I zoomed past the second, third, and fourth floor exits and yanked open the fifth-floor door.

I grabbed my board without slowing, feeling like my heart was going to blow up like a bomb inside my chest as I hurried down the hall.

I reached for my key card, but I didn't need it.

The door to 512 was cracked open.

Someone had broken into my motel room.

19

TUESDAY, 10:02 P.M.

TO SAY MY ROOM HAD BEEN TOSSED
was an understatement. The mattress was leaning up against
the wall, and the bottom was slashed open, stuffing sticking
out and everything. Same for the box spring: You could count
the coils. Dust bunnies fluttered around on the floor.

My clothes were strewn everywhere. Even the bath-
room was a mess—the little shampoo bottles lay empty on
the counter, with goo on the floor. The towels were trampled
near the toilet. These burglars had gone bananas.

For a second, I thought it might've been Ben, looking for
his box. But then I knew it had to be that cleaning lady and
her accomplice.

They wanted me to know they'd been here. Or at the very

least, they didn't care that I knew. Scratch that—they thought this was Ben's room. Not that it mattered at that moment.

I felt sick. Then I got scared. I backed out of my room, still clutching the box I'd just picked up. I thought of calling Agent Stark, Black, or even the White House Secret Service guys. But for some reason, I didn't want that. At least not right away.

First, I needed some advice from a friend.

"D*uuuu*de," Henry whispered when he saw the mess in my room. He stood outside, refusing to go past the threshold. Like maybe the bad guys could still get him.

"Crazy, huh?" I'd called him on his phone and found out that he was staying in the room next to me. Go figure. "So you didn't hear anything?"

Henry shrugged. "Some banging and stuff. But I thought maybe you were jumping on the bed."

"How old do you think I am?"

"What? The beds are bouncy. You couldn't blame a guy," Henry mumbled. "Did you call Stark yet?"

I shook my head. "I guess I'd better. But I have something I don't want her to know about." I grabbed the cardboard box that I'd set outside my room next to my skateboard and told Henry a little of the story.

When he heard about the Ben mix-up, he grinned and took the box to hide it in his room while I called Stark. It wasn't even five minutes later when she showed up at the door.

"What did you do?" Stark asked. She looked tired. But once she saw my room, she got worried instead. "Are you okay?"

"I'm fine. I wasn't here when they broke in."

"What did these people think they'd find?"

"Beats me." I shrugged. "They thought it was Ben's room. Maybe they don't like the guy either."

"I wonder if they thought you had the coat," Stark mumbled, ignoring my jab at Ben. "Is anything missing?"

I looked around, but with all the mess, it was hard to tell. "I don't know."

She moved around the room, then left to make a phone call. Once she got back, she had me gather my stuff, or what was left of it anyway. "You'll stay with Henry for now."

"Like a sleepover," Henry said, grinning. "This is awesome."

"I have a team coming over to take care of this," Agent Stark said. "And you're sure you didn't see anyone?"

"Positive," I said, lying through my teeth. I was dying for Stark to leave so I could check out that box already.

I wasn't sure why I didn't tell Stark I saw that cleaning lady and her sidekick. Maybe because I was embarrassed that I didn't recognize her before I went to the White House for dinner. And maybe because I wasn't sure if I could totally trust Pandora. My conversation with Ferguson had made me a bit paranoid.

Henry fake-yawned. "Gosh, I'm really tired, Agent Stark."

Stark squinted but then said, "You kids should get some

rest. Go on, I'll take care of things from here. Remember: We need to keep your and Ben's double status a secret. So keep a low profile."

"Sure, yeah." I quickly grabbed my pajamas and followed Henry to his room. Thankfully, he had two double-size beds. I'm all for rooming, but I like to have my own bed. On road trips, I have to share with Grandpa. He kicks in his sleep and yells stuff about his crime shows.

"Let's open the box," I said. We had about forty-four hours, and I could practically hear the bomb's timer tick-ticking away. It was like all those times I was late for school, riding my skateboard as fast as I could, knowing it was already past the second bell. Only this was much worse, considering the bomb could kill the president and Amy. And if the bad dude got hold of the Washington coat before we did, he could complete his plan. Get away without a scratch.

"Man, I'm dying to see what's inside," Henry said, handing me a pocketknife as we crouched by the box.

"I hope it's a clue. Some kind of lead." I put the box on the extra bed, which was now mine, and told him about the missing bomb.

Henry shook his head. "The bad guy has a bomb now? Man, it's getting worse by the minute. Let's get this box open and see if it'll help." He was crowding me to get a look inside.

"Give me some space." Last thing we needed was for me to slice Henry with his own pocketknife. I opened the flaps and removed some packing peanuts. There was a plastic bag that I tore open. Inside was dark blue wool. A cream-colored band of fabric, with brass buttons.

I ripped the plastic some more and pulled out a heavy coat.

"That's it," Henry whispered. "We found the Dangerous Double!"

You didn't think it would be that easy, right? Okay, so this *was* a coat, and it did look like the George Washington one from the picture Stark showed me. But there were no telltale burn marks where the bullets bounced off.

This wasn't the Dangerous Double.

"It's a replica," I said to Henry. At the bottom of the box was an invoice for Costumez-R-Us. Ben had paid eighty dollars for the coat and another forty for expedited shipping. "That's pricey for a fake."

"So why did Ben order this?" Henry asked.

"Who knows?" Angry and frustrated, I stuffed the coat back inside the box and pushed the package to the ground. "It's not the Dangerous Double; that's all that matters."

"Maybe he was trying to trick you," Henry said as he sat on his bed. "Pass that one off as the real thing."

I got on my bed, put my feet up, and shook my head. "Not his style. And I would find out anyway." I stretched out and got comfortable. This was a major bummer. Of course I'd hoped to find the Dangerous Double. I wanted it to be easy.

Once my initial frustration wore off, I began to think about Ben. "What was he planning to do with this coat?"

"Who knows? But you'll figure it out," Henry said as he got in bed. "You always do."

For everyone's sake, I hoped Henry was right.

"Do you think I could be a field agent?" Henry asked. "You know, go hunt down clues, like you?"

"Sure," I said, wondering where this came from. "Don't you like being the tech guy?"

"Of course I do." Henry was quiet for a moment. "But tech guys don't get invited for Taco Tuesdays with the president and her daughter."

He had a point. I turned off the lights. "Next time, you can be my guest."

"Okay." Henry sounded tired. He fell asleep almost right away. I could tell, because he did a soft wheezy thing in his sleep, like a leaky air mattress.

Me, I fell asleep not long after. And I dreamed of a ball at the White House, where everyone was wearing George Washington coats like the one Ben ordered. In the middle of the ballroom, there was a box. When I opened it, there was a ticking bomb inside.

Telling me to hurry up.

20

PLACE: HENRY'S MOTEL ROOM

TIME: WEDNESDAY, 8:00 A.M.

STATUS: ASLEEP

"LINC!" SOMEONE POKED MY CHEEK.

I opened my eyes. Henry's face was so close to mine, I could count the freckles.

What a way to wake up, huh?

"Dude, give me some space." I leaned on my elbows and realized I was still wearing my clothes from the day before. I was so tired, I'd forgotten to put on my pajamas. "What time is it?" The heavy motel curtains blocked out all the light, so there was no way to tell.

"Eight." Henry stepped back and dangled a paper bag in front of me. "Bagels and orange juice."

"Good." I sat up and rubbed my face. "Those plastic-wrapped rolls in the lobby could be lethal weapons. Might make a good gadget someday."

Henry snickered at that. He handed me my bag, then sat down to eat his own breakfast. "So did you get anywhere yesterday?"

Between bagel bites, I told him about my adventures with Amy: the International Spy Museum, the fish market, and how I was waiting for some super-secret spy to get in touch so I could track down the Culper Ring and whoever was keeping the Dangerous Double safe.

"Wow, you've been busy, huh?" Henry said.

"I should check to see if I got a message." I called down to the receptionist and asked.

"Yes, young man," the front desk lady answered before I even gave her my room number. "I'm sorry, but you have no messages."

I hung up, feeling like someone set off a firecracker in my stomach.

"You know, these spies always know how to find you," Henry said. "This person will get a message to you."

"How do you know?"

Henry blushed. "That's how it goes on TV, right?"

We both laughed at that.

"Hey, I just thought of something," Henry said. "You're not in your own room anymore—you're in mine. The receptionist probably looked under my room number since you called from here. What if the spy sent a message to your old room?"

"Henry, you're a genius."

"I know," he said with a grin.

I called the front desk, and after making the receptionist take my old room number down, she came back with my message.

"It's weird," she said. "Are you sure this is for you? You're a kid, right?'

"Just give it."

"'Lincoln is still for sale, but won't last. One thousand dollars. Cash only. No substitutes.'"

The receptionist was right: It really didn't make any sense. At all. I wrote the message down anyway.

After I hung up the phone, I showed the notepad to Henry.

"Are you buying a car?" he asked.

"No." I explained the ad I put in the newspaper.

"That's very old-school spy. Nowadays, we use the Internet for everything."

"So what does this message mean?"

"Lincoln—maybe that's you," Henry said as he looked at the Thrifty Suites Motel notepad.

"So I'm just a thousand bucks? That's a deal." Then I thought of something. "But I gave Ben's name, so that makes no sense. Abraham Lincoln was a president—maybe that's the White House or something?"

Henry shoved me in the shoulder. "The Lincoln Memorial!"

"Ouch." I rubbed my arm. Henry had a good punch for a scrawny kid. "That's right here in Washington, DC, so that makes sense. What about the rest?"

"*Lincoln is still for sale, but won't last.* That probably means this spy isn't going to wait for you." Henry pointed at the price. "Are you supposed to bring money? I mean, that's a lot."

"I don't know." I stared at the thousand dollars I'd written on the notepad. What twelve-year-old has that kind of cash? "What if it's not money? We have the place of the meeting—what if that's the time?"

"Ten o'clock!" Henry yelled really loud.

"Shhh! You know, you'd make a terrible spy," I said, but I was kind of excited, too. We'd cracked the message code.

"I'm the gadget guy for a reason." Henry pointed at the clock, which told me it was almost nine o'clock. "You might want to hustle."

"That Lincoln won't last."

21

WEDNESDAY, 9 A.M.

34 HOURS UNTIL THE BOMB

THIS LINCOLN WAS IN DESPERATE NEED
of a shower, so I rushed to clean up and change. I headed out
of Henry's room, passing room 512 on the way. The door was
closed, with no sign of the mess inside.

I took the stairs and rushed through the lobby—so fast
that I almost ran someone down. "Amy?"

She smiled, looking all fresh and rested and wearing her
red wig again. "In the flesh. It took you long enough to get
going." Amy gave me a frown. "You know I've been waiting
almost half an hour?"

"You're not supposed to be here," I said before I could
think. "Where's Steve anyway?"

"Outside." She pointed to the revolving door, where you could see glimpses of Steve's dark suit. "I told him I was showing my friend Ben around the city, which is sort of true. He offered to drive, but I figured walking is better. Easier to lose him, you know?" Amy grinned.

"Right." I tried to think of a way to lose her but couldn't come up with anything. I was about to meet some super-secret deep-cover spy, and I had the first daughter tagging along.

This was not good.

"Your shoes are untied again," I said.

Amy crouched down to fix the problem, looking kind of embarrassed.

"Your mom will be mad if she finds out you're coming along on the mission," I said. Lame argument, I know. But the girl was like Velcro.

"Mom thinks I'm just going to hang around the White House and study for four years—maybe even eight if she gets elected for a second term. I don't think so."

I didn't know what to say about that, so I let her walk outside with me.

"How'd you even know where I was staying?"

"Remember how Steve picked you up for dinner yesterday?" She shrugged. "I just asked him to take me to get you." Steve was still hanging back near the revolving door, looking like a doorman. "Now tell me where we're going."

As we walked away from the Thrifty Suites, I told her about the Lincoln Memorial and how Henry and I cracked the code. "So now we have to hurry."

"Before Ben gets wind of it." She was reading my mind—Ben could easily steal my plan, just like I'd stolen his package.

I stopped at the corner of the motel building. Steve stopped, too, standing about twenty feet behind us. "I need to figure out a way to slow Ben down," I said to Amy. A guy in a tracksuit passed us, talking on his cell phone.

Amy nodded. "Get him busted or something."

The guy with the phone gave me an idea. Something that worked for me in the past, something I'd done with Daryl and Sam when Sam's mom took away his Xbox and we were bored out of our minds. "Do you have a phone?"

"Of course." Amy dug into her pocket and pulled out her cell phone.

"Is your number traceable? Like with caller ID?"

"No. Secret Service set it up that way," Amy said, confirming what I'd hoped.

I pulled the piece of paper from my pocket, the one with everyone's phone number on it. I cleared my throat. Dialed Ben's number. But then my own phone rang in my pocket.

Huh?

I took a second to process how I could've called myself.

Ben and I had accidentally swapped phones.

It must've happened down in the clubhouse, when Wilson made all of us put our phones in the basket. That's why I got the call about the package—Ben had given the delivery company his number. I wasn't sure what to do with this information but figured I'd deal with it later.

"What's wrong?" Amy asked.

"Don't worry about it." I dialed my own number. And waited, one ring, two, three—

"Yes." Ben's voice was gruff, like he was just way too busy to answer the phone or something.

"Agent Green?" I asked in my lowest voice. Hoping he would fall for it. "This is the United States Secret Service."

Ben hesitated, like maybe he wasn't buying it. But then he answered, "Yessir. Please identify."

What was I supposed to say to that? "This is Agent, um, Steve. We need you to report to the White House immediately. Something has come up with the presidential mission."

"POTUS. Copy that, sir." Ben seemed to hesitate. "Have you notified other agents?" I almost cracked up. He was worried that I'd been called in, too.

"Negative," I said in my darkest tone of voice. "This notification is for you alone, Agent Green. Top secret. Wait in the White House staff kitchen until you are called in by, um, POTUS. Strictly confidential, eyes only." I might've overdone it with that last part.

But Ben bought it. "Copy, sir," he said in a fake deep and confident voice. "I will be there in thirty."

I hung up, because I couldn't keep from laughing any longer. And neither could Amy.

"Ben will be stuck there forever before he figures out he's been had," she said as we walked to the Lincoln Memorial. I hoped Amy was right about my phone call to Ben. "That was fun. I haven't made prank calls in a long time."

We zigzagged from street to street, passing one important-looking building after another. I was glad I had Amy with me. I had no idea where we were.

"We're here."

There was a big open plaza in front of the Lincoln Memorial, with small steps leading up to another level. Amy almost tripped over one as we walked up. The place looked like a Greek monument or something: white, with giant pillars at the entry. A wide stairway made it feel even more impressive. When I looked over my shoulder, I saw the Washington Monument off in the distance, with the Reflecting Pool stretching in front.

"Do you know what your contact looks like?" Amy asked, scanning the crowd.

"No clue," I answered. Tourists were everywhere, taking pictures of the Lincoln Memorial. Steve hung back, talking on his cell phone. It sounded like he was arguing with his girlfriend or something.

I followed Amy up the stairs, mostly because I didn't have a better idea. An old dude with a POW baseball cap sat on the third step. At the top, there was a giant stone chair with Abraham Lincoln sitting in it. "Whoa, someone really supersized the guy." My voice echoed off all the stone.

"Lincoln was a great president," a man said behind me. "Maybe the greatest that ever was. Or maybe that was Washington."

I turned around to look at the old man I saw on my way in. Up close, you could really see the wrinkles, the bushy gray hair. And I had a gut feeling.

This was the spy.

"I kind of like our current president," Amy said, jutting her chin. "Sometimes, a lady can do a better job, you know."

"History will tell," the spy dude grumbled. His eyes darted—to the stairs and the people that roamed the memorial. "You brought them." He cursed under his breath.

"Who?" Amy was annoyed. She still didn't get that this was our contact.

"One o'clock." Spy Guy glanced across the giant plaza in front of the Lincoln Memorial.

"That old lady?" Amy gave me a look.

"She's not old," Spy Guy said. "I'm guessing about thirty-five. Just a good disguise."

I squinted but didn't see how an old lady in a blue shirt with a quilted bird on it could be an agent in disguise.

"And at ten o'clock—that African American couple." Spy Guy huffed. "You brought them, too, didn't you?" He started to get super-stressed now. "This is a trap—I knew it!"

"Dude, calm down." I looked at Amy, but she was still trying to figure out how the African American couple in their jeans and wool coats could be spies. They acted like your usual tourists. "I think you're being paranoid," I told Spy Guy.

That got me the wickedest death ray of all time. He shoved me and started rushing down the stairs.

"Hey, wait!" Amy called.

Big mistake. People looked up. And that old lady, and the African American couple? They started moving. Following our man. He was right: They really were agents.

Spy Guy was running now, sending his POW cap flying. He was my only lead to the Dangerous Double—and he was getting away!

Without him, I had nothing.

So I ran after him.

22

"COME ON!" I PULLED AMY ALONG. WE raced after our spy, but he was pretty fast for an old guy. And since I had Amy with me, I couldn't use my skateboard.

We ran to the street behind the Lincoln Memorial. Steve was nowhere in sight. By the time we caught up with our guy, he was already in an old beat-up truck, ready to drive away.

Amy and I didn't stop until we reached the truck. I looked over my shoulder but didn't see the people who'd been following us. Not yet, anyway. I tapped the passenger-side window.

Spy Guy shook his head.

I moved in front of the truck and gave him my best death-ray stare as I leaned on the rusty hood. I wasn't about to let my only lead get away. And I really hoped he wasn't into running down twelve-year-old kids.

Spy Guy looked miffed but then waved for us to get inside. Once we got in the backseat, he barked, "Get down!"

His truck smelled like old socks and wet dog. Newspapers littered the floor and the seats.

"Cover up." Spy Guy tossed a hairy blanket over us, and I thought I was going to gag. It was a good thing Amy's hair smelled like apples, because otherwise, I think I might've just taken off. This truck was seriously gross. Spy Guy started the engine, and it made a roaring noise as he pushed the gas. He cursed.

"What's wrong?" I called from under the blanket.

"They got themselves a car," Spy Guy said. "Hold on. This is gonna get bumpy." I was expecting him to speed, but he just puttered down the street, leaving a black plume as his only trail.

With the blanket over my head, I snuck a peek out the rear window. Traffic was light enough for me to spot the African American couple in a sedan, just a few cars behind the truck.

"Hang tight," Spy Guy said over his shoulder.

Suddenly, he turned right—*hard*. Sending me and Amy flying in the back. A sharp left threw us to the other side. And just as I tried to look out the back again, he slammed the brakes, so my head jerked back.

We'd stopped in some sort of alleyway, behind a Dumpster.

"Did you lose them?" I asked, rubbing my forehead.

"Think so. We'll hang here another minute, to be safe."

Spy Guy pulled at his hair and took off a wig, revealing a gray-haired crew cut. Then he peeled back a layer of wrinkly skin and looked a whole lot younger. He still looked old—fifty or sixty, but no longer ancient.

"Who are you?" Amy asked. She straightened her wig, tucking a blond curl back under it. "You don't look like a spy."

"That's the idea," he said. "I'm John Smith." Sounded like a fake name, but okay.

"Benjamin Green," I said.

John Smith laughed. "No, you're not. You're his look-alike, Lincoln Baker."

He knew. I didn't know what to say, plus the stink in the truck was overwhelming. I tried to crack the window open, but the handle was gone.

"The auto mechanic's son," John Smith said with a nod. He started the truck back up, and we drove out of the alley. "Should be safe now."

"How do you know about Ben and me being look-alikes and about my dad's shop?" I asked Smith.

"I still have my contacts, and I like to keep an eye on Pandora. But don't worry—your double status is still a well-kept secret." We'd now left the city and were driving on a highway lined with trees. "So you're on a new mission, huh?"

"It's fun," Amy said cheerfully.

Smith gave her a sharp look in the rearview. "This isn't some game, *missy.* These agents you're toying with wouldn't hesitate to come to your house and kill you in your sleep—heck, they can make it so you never even existed."

Amy looked like someone had just slapped her in the face.

"Take it easy, man," I said.

Smith clutched the steering wheel. "You kids have no idea who you're dealing with." He took a deep breath to calm down. "You don't know what it's like, always looking over your shoulder."

"Actually, I know exactly what that's like," Amy said, her voice trembling. "There's always Secret Service everywhere—and now there's someone who wants my family dead." She was scared after all.

"Threats to the president are normal," Smith grumbled.

"This time is different." Amy told him about the bomb and how the bad dudes were planning to use the Dangerous Double. I probably could've stopped her from sharing top secret information. But I figured Smith was so paranoid and secretive, he'd never tell anyone. And he seemed to know everything anyway, so I decided just to show him all my cards. "We need your help finding the George Washington coat. Before these bad guys do."

"Frank at the fish market told us you could get us in touch with the Culper Ring."

Smith didn't talk for a long time. "I never thought this day would come," he said eventually.

"What day?" I asked.

"The day I would give up the Culper Ring book."

23

WEDNESDAY, 11:00 A.M.

32 HOURS UNTIL THE BOMB

"THERE'S A BOOK?" I ASKED.

"No more talking!" Smith barked. "I'll tell you nothing else, not until we're safe."

Amy looked behind her through the grimy window. "They're not following us anymore."

"Oh, they're not far behind, believe me. The agents always find you if you don't keep moving." Smith tapped his temple and stepped on the gas. "They get into your head."

We drove straight for a while longer, until the truck lurched right and Smith took an exit off the highway and got on a narrow road into the woods.

Me, I was just hungry, and I was trying to avoid breathing

in the stinky truck. Amy seemed down and a little scared. John Smith kept humming a tune to himself—"Three Blind Mice."

"Where are we going, exactly?" I asked after nothing but dense forest zoomed by for about twenty minutes. Mom would freak if she knew what I was doing: in a strange truck with an even stranger dude, riding to the middle of nowhere.

But I was on a mission.

"I would take you to where you need to go," Smith said, "but I gotta pack up my stuff and clear out with my trailer. Before they catch up with me."

"Who?" Amy asked. She grabbed my arm as the truck barreled over rocky gravel. We needed to leave this crazy train.

Smith slowed down and pulled into a deserted campground. He drove all the way to the farthest spot and backed the truck up to a lone trailer. It was an Airstream—like a silver submarine on wheels. They were huge in the fifties and sixties. I know, because Grandpa used to own one.

Smith shut the engine off. It sputtered a fat cloud of black smoke and was quiet. He checked his watch. "I figure we have ten minutes to get out of here. Before those agents catch up. You kids can go now if you want. There's a bus stop three clicks east of here."

"Three clicks?" Was that crazy spy-speak for something?

"That's three kilometers," Amy whispered. "About two miles."

Two miles of walking? No thanks. Plus, I had to see this

through, creepy guy or not. "You promised to help," I said as we all got out of the truck. "I want to hear about the Culper Ring and this book."

Smith didn't answer. Instead he started to whistle. A scrappy little terrier came running for us, barking like a mad dog.

I jumped in front of Amy. But then the dog mellowed out. He sat down at my feet, wagging his tail.

"Take it easy, Nixon." Smith rubbed the dog's head and pulled a treat from his pocket. "Don't worry about him," Smith said to me. "I got Nixon as a guard dog, but so far he's just loved people to death."

Amy was already all over Nixon, and he was happy to make a new friend.

"We just left Steve hanging back there," I whispered to her. "Is that going to get you in trouble?"

Amy shook her head. "He'll be too embarrassed and worried about getting in trouble himself. I'll send him a text to tell him I'm okay."

Smith grabbed a wrench from a toolbox in the truck bed, gave me a set of pliers, and motioned for me to follow him. "We can talk while I hook the trailer to the hitch."

"So who's part of this Culper Ring?" I handed Smith the pliers. He leaned over the hitch and undid a pin.

Smith wore a key on a chain around his neck. It dangled as he pulled the trailer and hooked it to the truck. Then he put the pin back in, securing it.

Smith gave me the pliers again. "I have no idea, to tell you the truth. I only have bits of information. I'm just one link in the chain—you get what I'm saying?" He wiped his hands on an old rag. "But I can tell you where to find the information to help you find this person. You—" Smith froze as his eyes drifted to the distance.

"What?" I followed his gaze, but all I saw was the road to the campground and lots of trees.

"They found me," he mumbled.

Amy joined us with Nixon. "What's wrong?"

Smith pointed. "Headlights, up ahead. We gotta go. Now!"

Amy, Nixon, and I jumped in the backseat of the truck, and Smith wasted no time punching the gas to get up to speed. Behind us, the trailer wobbled back and forth. Nixon moved to the passenger seat, looking confused over all the excitement.

"Now tell me about this Culper Ring book," I said to Smith. We needed that information, whatever paranoid craziness was going on inside his head.

"Today's Culper Ring agents don't know each other— just like with the old Culper Ring during the Revolutionary War." Smith stroked Nixon's head, and the dog settled down in the passenger seat. "But now, they do communicate with each other, unlike in the past—that's how you were able to get to me. There are just layers of security. So secrets can't be exposed by one bad link."

"Where do I find the agent who has the Dangerous Double?" I asked, feeling like I was about to get my big answer.

Smith pulled onto the main road, and the trailer rocked violently behind us. "To find the name of the agent, you'll need the Culper Ring book. It has the numbers of the spies and their real names—the old Culper Ring used a similar book to keep track of agents. The new Culper Ring has one, too."

"Where's the Culper Ring book?" Amy asked.

"A deep-cover agent found it some time ago. I heard he hid it," Smith said.

"Where?" Amy and I asked at the same time.

Smith exhaled. "I don't think you'll be able to get to it."

"Why not?" I asked.

Smith smiled. "It's at Langley, CIA headquarters. In room 355, taped to the back of the bottom drawer of the far left filing cabinet. Right under their noses. But there's no way you—get down!"

24

"STAY DOWN!" SMITH YELLED.

Amy and I slid to the floor. In the rearview mirror, I could see Smith's darting eyes, making him look like even more of a Froot Loop.

"What's happening?" I whispered.

"He's crazy, that's what," Amy mumbled next to me.

"They're going toward the campground, those government pawns from before—I told you they were coming! The agents, Nixon," Smith said. The dog sat up when he heard his name. His tail was wagging, slapping against the back of the seat. "They found us."

Nixon would agree with anything. If you told him aliens were coming from Mars, he would wag his tail, too. He was a dog.

Smith sighed. "I know what you kids think. What every-one thinks." He stroked his dog's head. "But when the doo-doo hits the fan, they all come talking to that wacko Smith."

The guy was right. Here we were, crouched down on the nasty floor mats of his stinky truck—and Smith had been the best lead so far. Now we knew where to find the book that identified who had the Dangerous Double.

"Can we sit back in the seat now?" I asked. "My leg is cramping majorly over here."

"Sure," Smith said.

Looking at the old trailer in the rearview mirror, I real-ized something. "*You* hid the book at Langley."

Smith hesitated, but then he nodded.

"Can't you just tell us who has the Dangerous Double?" Amy asked.

Smith laughed. "I told you kids, links in a chain. I never read it—that would give me too much information, here." He tapped the side of his head. "You'll need the book to find the name. That's the only way."

Through the grimy window of Smith's truck, I watched the trees fly by and tried to imagine how we'd get inside CIA headquarters.

"The Culper Ring knows someone bad is after the coat," Smith said. "Whoever has the Dangerous Double will be expecting you and will be ready to give it to Pandora for safe-keeping. But you'll need the book to show you're the good guys, you know what I'm saying?"

"Like the dollar with Frank," I said. "So why is the CIA

after you?" I asked Smith.

"Who says they're after me, Young Abe?"

"Young Abe?"

"He means Abraham Lincoln," Amy whispered to me. "You know, the sixteenth president, and your name is—"

"I get it, Amy," I said through gritted teeth.

"The agents are always out to squash the truth." Smith banged his dashboard, making Nixon whimper. "Sorry, Nix." He petted his dog.

"Well, thanks a lot for your help," I said. I felt frustrated over the whole CIA headquarters business but knew I wasn't going to get any more answers from Smith.

Right then, my phone rang, and really loud, too. I scrambled to pull it from my coat pocket. I checked the number. It was Ben, calling from my Pandora phone—probably ready to read me the riot act on the prank phone call I made that morning.

I picked up. "Ben?"

"Baker," he whispered. "You set me up!"

"I have no idea what you're talking about," I fibbed.

"You sent me to the White House on a fake assignment and—never mind," he hissed. "I caught on. Now I am at the Smithsonian. I need backup."

Before I could answer, Smith reached back and pulled the phone from my hands. "You have a mobile phone?" he spat, like it was anthrax or something.

"Yeah." I reached for it, but Smith was too fast.

"These things are beacons for the enemy, don't you get

it?" Smith looked like he was going to kill me.

"Okay, chill. I'll turn it off." I grabbed it from him.

"It doesn't matter." I thought Smith's head was going to explode or something. "They can track you with those things even when they're off. Don't you get why I live like I do—no phones, no computers, no credit cards?"

I was afraid to say anything.

"Off the grid," Amy whispered.

"The grid is how they get to you. How they *own* you." Smith pulled over. "You need to go, both of you. Now!"

I slid up on the seat to find that we were back in DC again, which was a good thing. "Fine. Thanks for the ride."

Smith grumbled.

"How do we find you?" I asked as I got out.

"You don't." Smith hesitated. "I'll be around a few more days. If you're in trouble, I'll find you."

"Well, thanks." I barely closed the door before Smith pulled away. The silver trailer rocked as he swerved back into traffic.

"That guy's seriously paranoid," I said to Amy.

"I like his dog." She waved to the truck as it disappeared, like Smith would actually appreciate her niceness. Then she sighed. "I should probably call Steve."

"If he hasn't called in a SWAT team by now," I joked.

But Amy wasn't smiling when she dialed his number. And I could hear him yelling even though I was a good ten feet away. Amy was in deep, deep trouble.

* * *

122

We met him in front of the Lincoln Memorial—at least it was a public place, so he couldn't make too much of a scene. Steve was about to blow up when Amy cut him off.

"I'm fine," Amy said. "We just met up with a . . . *friend*."

Steve ran his fingers through his hair. "I almost called in an Amber Alert, you know. Next time, I'm calling your mother! Forget this protection detail—you're impossible to keep safe." He looked seriously miffed.

"I'm sorry," Amy said, sounding nervous. Maybe she'd pushed Steve too far by taking off with John Smith. "I really am."

After a long pause, Steve straightened his jacket. "Okay, apology accepted." He pointed at her. "But this is the *last time* I'm covering for you, you understand?" He looked at me. "And you, too, young man."

Amy smiled and brushed back her fake red hair. "Sure thing, Steve. Thanks for being so great." She started walking toward the Lincoln Memorial, and I followed.

Things were back to normal. Steve trailed his usual distance of a dozen feet behind us, but this time he felt a lot like a dark cloud that was about to dump a bunch of rain.

Amy kept talking. "John Smith's right, you know."

"What—about his anti-phone attitude?" I waited for years to get a phone. What's his issue?

"All the technology we use makes it very easy to find us," Amy said. She buttoned her coat at the neck. There was dog hair all over it. "We shop on the computer, post our pictures, send messages. . . . It's like a trail of bread crumbs for someone to follow if they want."

Right then my phone—or Ben's phone, technically—
started buzzing

"Ben's texting from the Smithsonian," I said.

SOS.

25

FOR THE RECORD: I DIDN'T WANT TO SAVE

Benjamin Green. If it had been up to me, I would've let him wait it out. It was his fault he didn't take any of Henry's gadgets, right?

You agree with me, I know.

But Amy didn't. "What if his life is in danger?"

"Ben's fine. He can fight his way out. Maybe he can hit the bad dudes on the head with his junior agent manual."

"You don't mean that." Amy gave me a disapproving look. "SOS—it doesn't get any clearer than that."

"He'll be fine," I repeated.

"Well, I'm going over to help him anyway. You just don't leave someone when they ask you for help." Amy walked away, leaving me standing there.

Steve ignored me and crossed the street behind her. He'd be no good in an emergency, that was for sure.

I had to go with Amy to protect her. I sighed. Then I started to sprint. "Wait up, Amy!"

The Smithsonian—now that sounds like one museum, right? Turns out that it isn't. The Smithsonian is actually an institute, a whole conglomeration of museums spread around the National Mall in Washington, DC. Dad could spend a week there and still not see everything.

"So how do we even know where to look?" I asked Amy, who had kind of taken charge of this Save Ben mission.

We were walking down Constitution Avenue, with the Washington Monument to our right, which was crawling with tourists. To our left, I caught a glimpse of the White House in the distance, reminding me I was running out of time to find the coat. And now I had to save Ben—talk about a waste of time.

"I don't know."

Amy stopped and looked at me. "Didn't he tell you where he was?" Steve hung back a little farther, and he seemed really wrapped up in a cell phone conversation. For Amy's sake, I hoped he wasn't ratting her out to her mom.

"The Smithsonian, that's it." I had tried to call Ben after the text, but it went straight to voice mail. Not a good sign.

Amy bit her lip and frowned. "You know, they keep the real George Washington uniform on display here at the

American History Museum. It's part of this exhibit on war. Could the Dangerous Double be there, too?"

It all made sense now: Ben's package, the replica of the coat. "When we were on our mission in Paris, we found the evil *Mona Lisa* in a gift shop at the Louvre. Hiding in plain sight."

"And Ben thinks that's where the George Washington Dangerous Double is?" Amy thought about that for a second. "I guess it's possible."

"Maybe." Truth was, I really didn't want Ben to be right and win our bet. "But our Dangerous Double had marks from the bullets, remember? Does the coat on display have that?"

"I don't remember," Amy said.

We took a right on 14th, then a left on Madison Drive, with the grass of the National Mall stretching to our right. I wondered if Ben could be on track after all. And if that was why he'd ordered that coat: to swap it with the Dangerous Double.

But I had his package, so why was he here at the Smithsonian? We stood in front of the American History Museum now. Steve hung back far and wasn't really paying attention to us. From a quick glance at his cell phone screen, I was pretty sure he was playing Flying Chickens. Way to be sharp on the job, Steve.

"Let's go see if we can find Ben," Amy said. "I'll tell Steve we're going inside so he doesn't get all freaked out. She hurried over, and after they exchanged a few words, we left him on the grass of the National Mall.

I stopped her at the door. "Give me your hat and glasses."

Amy smiled. "A disguise—smart move."

The hat was itchy and the glasses felt kind of tight behind my ears, but I figured it was temporary. Last thing I needed was for these bad dudes to home in on me.

"You definitely look different," Amy said, studying me.

I scratched at my neck. "Let's hurry already."

Inside, there was a big entry hall with white stone floors. As I turned around, I could see an upper level of the museum. A big banner advertising Celebrating America's History Week hung above the banister, with a picture of (you guessed it) George Washington at its center.

Entry to the American History Museum was free, and they even let me bring in my backpack—good news, because I still didn't know how we were going to rescue Ben. My Henry gadgets might come in handy.

"The coat is on the third floor," Amy said, showing the spot on the map once we made it past security. "We came in on the second floor, see?"

It was a little confusing, but I saw from the map that she was right—there was a level below ours. We were in Flag Hall, which was the second floor. I turned around again and saw a giant American flag on display behind a wall of glass.

"So we need to go to the third floor," Amy said.

I hesitated. "What if it's a trick?"

"From Ben?" That's what I'd been thinking, but when she said it, I shook my head. "He wouldn't be that smart. I'm thinking more of bad dudes. Think about it: We were followed—to the fish market, the memorial, and in the truck. I'm sure Ben has been, too. And I'll bet that's why he called: He needs us to shake his tail." That sounded kind of gross, but you get what I meant, right?

"The George Washington coat is in the Price of Freedom exhibit—section eight on the east side," Amy said, pointing at the number eight on the map. "If we were just visiting, I'd take that elevator right up to section eight."

"But that's dangerous."

Amy nodded. "You come right up by the Price of Freedom exhibit. Where Ben sent his SOS message."

It would be too easy for the bad guys to spot us. If they had Ben trapped, they were probably near that elevator. Looking at the map more closely, I said, "Let's go to the west wing of the museum and sneak across."

Amy folded the map. "What do we do once we get there?" We walked across the floor to the west wing of the museum.

"I have a plan." I pulled the black knit cap over my ears.

Okay, so maybe I didn't *exactly* have a plan. But then that wasn't a first for me. Sometimes you have to let the plan come to you. And that's what I was doing as we rode the west side elevator to the third floor. I was waiting for an opportunity.

"What is the plan?" Amy whispered next to me.

"I'll find out when we get up there."

"That's *so* not a plan." Amy shook her head as we got off the elevator.

"Shoelaces, Amy," I said to distract her. "Double knots."

She crouched down to tie them.

When she finished, I said, "Let's hurry up. For all we know, those guys could make their move any second now."

On the third floor, there were several closed-off exhibits on the left and bathrooms to the right. A hall led past the restrooms, toward the east side of the museum, where Ben was.

"Let's try to get closer to the exhibit," I said to Amy. Using a group of tourists to hide behind, we passed the restroom area and got to the banister on the left that overlooked Flag Hall below.

"Section eight is straight ahead," Amy said.

I pushed the fake glasses up my nose and peered around the woman walking in front of me.

Amy followed my cue. "I don't see any bad guys."

"Maybe they're not wearing their bad dude badges today," I said.

Amy snickered. "Okay, point taken. But how do we spot them, then?" We passed the banister and neared the exhibit.

"We'll have to go in and find Ben," I said. From looking at the map, I knew there was only one way in and out of the exhibit. And I wondered if that's how Ben got himself trapped.

As we went inside, I seriously thought of calling the whole thing off. To be honest, part of me was hoping the bad guys would go for it. Have them take Benjamin Green. But then there was the other part of me, the part that heard Mom at the back of my head. Telling me I needed to be nice. That part of me knew I had to do the right thing.

"So where's Ben?" Amy asked. We passed a helicopter (really) with a pilot mannequin inside. I tried to see if I could spot any bad guys, but there were too many clusters of tourists.

"I don't know." The place was dimly lit, making it hard to see beyond the crowds gathering around the exhibit pieces. "Let's find the coat; maybe he's there. Just . . ." I glanced around.

"Watch out for bad guys, I know," Amy said.

We saw a jeep, dangling above some signs with informative stuff on them. I was trying to find Ben and scram already. The worst thing? This rescue mission was a distraction from my search for the coat.

"The coat is over there," Amy said, pointing between the clusters of museum visitors. George Washington's uniform—that blue coat with the cream trim—was behind a glass display. But I didn't see Ben.

Amy walked toward the uniform exhibit, but before I could follow, I heard someone call my name.

"Hey, Linc!" I heard a person hiss behind me. I turned around and saw Ben. Crouched down, hiding behind the helicopter exhibit, looking stressed out.

I joined him. "Where are the bad dudes?" I asked as I crouched down, too.

I saw that Ben had a little smile on his face. And it wasn't a friendly one. He reached out and snatched the hat and glasses off my head.

"Wait!" I said, probably a little too loud. I jumped up.

But he was already off, wearing the hat and glasses. Amy was right: It was a very effective disguise.

"What's he doing?" Amy had rushed over. "Why is he running away?"

I had a gut feeling. Thought I knew why Ben left. "Never mind that. We need to get out of here!"

But as I turned around to find our way out, I saw them: a guy in an expensive-looking navy sports jacket, standing near a cannon. And another dude, wearing a black sweater that was tight over his muscular arms, standing by the jeep display. They both wore sensible secret agent shoes—a dead giveaway they were agents. But bad dude agents. They both had their eyes on me.

These were the bad guys Ben was trying to escape.

I could see the exhibit exit. And I saw Ben in his disguise as he was leaving, turning to look at me. Saluting me on his way out.

"What's he doing?" Amy asked.

My gut was right. "He's setting me up."

26

IT WAS PAYBACK FOR MY PRANK PHONE
call. I knew that now. Ben saw an opportunity to stick it to
me, and he took it.

My blood boiled, but then I spotted the two bad guys
coming our way. And I was without my disguise. A sitting
duck.

I clenched my fists. But I quickly realized that there was
no time to be angry.

"Now what?" Amy whispered, spotting the guys, too.

"Now we run," I said. "You first."

Amy hesitated, but only for a nanosecond. She rushed
toward the exit, using the clusters of visitors to hide.

I was frozen. The bad guys were now walking together

and were just ten feet away. I had to move. *Fast.*

So I did the only thing I could think of. I stepped away from the helicopter. And ran right for them.

They looked confused.

I sidestepped them, darting away just fast enough to keep them from grabbing me. Sometimes, being a kid comes in handy. I rushed toward the exit, knowing that my move would only give me a slight advantage.

I rushed out of the Price of Freedom exhibit just in time to watch Amy disappear behind closing elevator doors to my left.

I ran right, back to the way we came in. My ears were buzzing, and it seemed like I could hear everything just a little better.

People laughing. A whining toddler.

I rushed for the elevator on the west side, hoping I was faster than the bad guys. But when I looked ahead, it was like a wall of people over there. There was a cluster of more than a dozen visitors, waiting to go down.

This was not good.

The bad guys were coming up behind me.

I was stuck.

Then I saw an opening. The banister to my right, overlooking Flag Hall below. It was a bad idea, I knew that. But sometimes, a bad idea is all you've got.

I started to walk over to the banister. My heart was pounding, and I felt the eyes of the bad guys on me. They were just twenty feet away now.

I unzipped the bottom pocket of my backpack and pulled out the blowup boat.

I yanked the cord as I ran to the banister.

"Hey, kid, what are you doing?" someone yelled behind me.

I tossed the blown-up boat over the ledge, to the floor below. I climbed on the banister, clutching the Celebrating America's History Banner hanging from strings above me, and hesitated.

It was a long, *long* way down.

Then I felt the banner's string come loose to the left. And to the right.

So I closed my eyes.

And I jumped.

27

WEDNESDAY, 1:30 P.M.

AMY WAS RIGHT. DON'T TRY THIS AT home, in case you have some blowup boat in your garage. It was a lot like the time Daryl and I tried these cool new skateboard moves—at least I'd learned how to take a fall, which came in handy as I crawled to my feet. I'd banged my elbow. *Hard*. But the rest of me was okay.

I hurried to untangle myself from the banner—George Washington was right in my face, if you can believe it. Then, leaving my blowup boat (sorry, Smithsonian), I rushed out of the museum without a hitch.

It was a miracle, honestly.

Amy was already outside with Steve. As I walked up, I could hear bits and pieces of conversation. Bottom line:

Steve was fed up with Amy's antics. He was making her walk double time back to the motel so he could get his car. And I couldn't help but feel guilty. If it wasn't for me, she wouldn't be running all over the place.

"That Ben is a piece of work!" Amy whispered, shaking her head, looking miffed.

Me, I was ready to run the guy over with my skateboard. I was so mad I couldn't speak.

Luckily, Amy was talking enough for the both of us. "We could have been captured by the bad guys. Imagine that! Kidnapped—maybe they would have put us in a dungeon. Interrogated us until we gave up the Dangerous Double."

"We don't have it, remember?" I practically spat at Amy. But then I saw her shocked expression, and I chilled out. "Sorry. I guess I kind of had it coming, after that phone prank."

"That's not exactly the same thing," Amy argued. We stopped at E Street, waiting to cross. "You didn't send him evil guys."

"I'll get him back," I said. But as we crossed the street, the cold wind chilled my boiling temper. And I thought of my mission—I had to find the Dangerous Double.

We walked for ten more minutes to get back to the motel. Amy went on about all the ways the bad guys could have made our lives miserable—I think she might be a crime show fan, like Grandpa. I sort of tuned her out, though. I tried to focus and think of how I was going to get the Culper Ring book.

But when we were back at the Thrifty Suites, I still had no

plan to get inside the CIA.

Steve was motioning Amy to the car. We parted and promised to meet in front of the White House at five.

Standing in the Thrifty Suites lobby, I realized that I was pretty hungry. And I wanted some advice on this mission, so I called Henry.

"Perfect timing," Henry said when I suggested food. "I sort of skipped lunch, and I'm starving." He told me to meet him outside the White House visitor center.

I skateboarded over there, finding Henry by a food truck with a wiener dog painted on it. He was third in line.

"Hot dogs for dinner?" I asked as I strapped my skateboard to my backpack.

Henry nodded. "Look at this line!" He pointed to the dozen or so people behind him. "If it's this busy, it must be good."

Now, I wasn't so sure about that. But this was probably my only chance to have dogs for dinner, since Mom is real particular about my nutrition and all. "Why not?" I said. I ordered a drink and one hot dog.

Henry ordered four. "What?" he said when I gave him a look. "I'm having a growth spurt."

We sat down on the edge of a concrete planter in front of the visitor center. "So how's the mole hunt going?" I took a bite of my hot dog.

Henry swirled the ice in his soda cup. "We're getting nowhere. And Agent Stark is all cranky—you ever get the feeling she hates kids?"

"Try sitting next to her on a five-hour flight." I took another bite of my dog.

Henry went on to tell me how they were looking at security footage from the White House. "But we're coming up empty. This guy is just too good, you know?" He chewed on his food for a minute. "It's almost like the mole is an expert at being a mole. Does that make sense?"

"No. But then, not a lot of this case does." I told Henry about Ben setting me up, which made him choke on his hot dog. Then I told him about John Smith and the whole Culper Ring business.

"So who has the Dangerous Double?"

"Shhh!" I looked around, but the tourists were too busy taking pictures, studying maps, and eating hot dogs to care about our conversation. "We have to find the Culper Ring book to find out who has the coat."

"Your mission sounds a lot like our hunt for the mole," Henry said. "Confusing."

"There's this Culper Ring, a secret book, and all these agents that are after us like we're the bad guys. It's like a puzzle with a ton of pieces, but none of them fit together," I said.

"When I do a puzzle, I always look at the picture on the box," Henry said.

"Only we don't have the box right now." This hot dog dinner conversation was beginning to depress me.

Henry polished off his last dog and belched. "Maybe I'll get another one. I'm still kind of hungry."

My phone buzzed. There was a text from Ben:

MEET ME AT HENRY'S LAB ASAP.

He was one of those all-caps texters who didn't get that was just like yelling. And I felt like giving him my all-caps reply—only in person. I clenched my jaw and got up, wiping the crumbs off my pants. "I need to meet with Ben. Catch you later, Henry."

Henry tossed out the trash and got back in line. "Let him have it."

"Oh, I will." I walked through the visitor center, toward the elevator. Inside, it was nice and quiet.

I made my way to Henry's lab above the White House visitor center. I'd get my phone and maybe whack Ben with my skateboard on the way out.

When I got to Henry's lab in room 418, Ben stood behind the desk like he owned the place. He uncrossed his arms, dug into his cargo pocket, and put the phone on the table.

I slammed his phone on the desk. "There's yours." I pulled my hand away, clenching into a fist.

Ben smiled. "I had to retaliate after that phone prank you pulled. You must know that." He tossed me Amy's hat and red glasses. "Thanks for the great cover."

I put the disguise in my backpack. "Well, your brilliant plan didn't work." It was my turn to dish out a smug smile. "I used one of Henry's gadgets to escape—the ones you were too good for, remember?"

Ben squinted.

"You know, you almost got the first daughter—how

would you say it—captured by the enemy?"

The smugness disappeared from his face. "How . . . ?"

"She was with me. Thankfully, she got out in one piece," I said. I grabbed my phone off the table. It felt cold and different, even though it was the exact same model as the one I'd been using.

Ben leaned on the desk. "Are you fraternizing with the first daughter?"

I couldn't really deny that, since I just threw Amy's presence at the Smithsonian in his face.

"I would advise against putting her in harm's way. The mission is far too dangerous for civilians." He picked up his phone. "Thank you for saving me back at the Smithsonian."

"You're *not* welcome."

Ben clenched his jaw. "Well, I suppose we're even now."

"Huh." I was still too mad to call a truce or anything. I took a breath to relax.

Ben hesitated. "You are a better junior agent than I thought."

I was. But this wasn't the time to gloat. Like it or not, I had to share my suspicions with Ben. "I've been wondering something," I said, holding my phone. "Those guys at the Smithsonian."

"Ex-CIA," Ben said. "The clothes, the aggressiveness— they all point to contract agents. Not government. These guys somehow tracked me to the museum."

"I've been followed, too." First, to the fish market. Then there were those agents at the Lincoln Memorial. I was beginning to put the pieces together. "Mine were actual agents."

"CIA, active agents?"

I thought of what Frank Two said and John Smith. "I'm pretty sure."

Ben frowned. "But *we* are CIA. Why are they following us?"

"I don't know why." Maybe John Smith was right. "I do know *how* they're following us."

Ben gave me a skeptical frown. "How?"

"They're tracking us by our cell phones."

28

BEN CLOSED HIS EYES AND SHOOK HIS head. "Of course, why didn't I think of this?"

"So now what? Should we throw them out?"

Ben popped the back cover off his phone. "No. You'll need to remove the battery." He did, and I followed. "We won't be able to use our phones, only in case of absolute emergency."

"The CIA, these ex-agent dudes . . . Why would they be tracking us?"

Ben frowned and tucked his phone in his pocket. "Pandora is black ops—deep undercover. Maybe they were not notified of our mission."

I put my phone away, too. But I didn't buy that whole black ops excuse. These people seemed to think *we* were the bad guys.

"Very well," Ben said. "We'll resume our mission to find the Dangerous Double."

"That's right," I said, ready to get back to the mission. I leaned on the desk so my face was close to Ben's. "And the next time you try to set me up, I'll use a Sure Shot *and* a Ruckus on a Roll on you."

He looked confused.

I stepped back. "If you showed Henry some respect, you'd know what I'm talking about."

"Fine," Ben said. He crossed his arms. "Our bet is still on. I find the coat, I get the medal."

"You're forgetting that *I'll* be the one finding the coat," I retorted.

Ben squinted. "May the best junior agent win."

"Right." Because we all knew the best agent was me, right?

I thought of a dozen excuses to give Amy for why we wouldn't break into the CIA. But they were all pretty lame. So I did something horrible.

I stood her up.

Then, I used the office phone on the desk in Henry's lab to see if he would come.

"Where are we going?" Henry asked. He sounded way too excited—probably because he'd get to be a field agent.

"You'll see."

"Is it part of the mission? Did you find the *c-o-a-t*?"

"I'm sure if any bad guys are listening in, they know how to spell."

"Right." Henry snickered.

I told Henry I'd meet him outside the visitor center and went downstairs, feeling kind of guilty about ditching Amy. I tried to tell myself I was keeping her safe, but I still felt terrible.

When I got outside, Henry was already there, waving wildly, smiling. He was the opposite of secret. A few passing tourists were giving him a sideways glance. Then a black SUV pulled up. Henry gave me his proudest smile. "I even got us a ride and everything."

I was about to explain to Henry what the secret in secret agent was all about when the rear window of the SUV rolled down. Amy leaned out. "You ready to go?"

So much for me standing her up.

"She drove right by the visitor center," Henry said, all exited. "Cool, huh?"

I pulled Henry's arm. "This is a really bad idea. The mission is supposed to be secret. We can't have the Secret Service along, dude."

"How else are we going to get there—on our bikes? It's in Langley; that's half an hour's drive from here, you know."

Henry had a point.

"Fine. But Steve parks far away from the CIA building."

Henry shrugged. "Sure. You're such a worrywart, you know that?"

My friend Sam is really good at basketball and pretty much any other sport. So when it's time to pick teams in PE, he's a top choice. Daryl is your last option because he monkeys around too much. Me, I'm your middle pick: no jock, but I can surprise you when I put my mind to it. I'm the wild card.

Our team of CIA burglars? We were your last-pick crowd. Amy was chattering all excited. Henry was gazing at her with a weird twinkle in his eye. And I was beginning to feel a disaster was waiting for us at Langley.

At least Steve was oblivious, with the little divider window up. Apparently Amy told him we were stopping by Langley because Henry wanted to see what CIA headquarters looked like. She told him her mom set it up and he believed her. Steve was kind of a sucker.

But his Secret Service badge got us past the gatehouse. Then he parked at the far end of the parking lot.

"Has anyone thought about how we're going to break into the CIA?" I asked when we were on our own. "I mean, the place has to be like a fortress, right? You don't just walk in there and ask to search the file cabinet in room 355."

"Can't you call your boss to get you clearance?" Amy asked.

I shook my head. "I don't want them to be in on what we're doing. For all we know, the mole will hear what we're up to." Good guys, bad guys—there was no way to tell who was on which team. Better to keep everything to ourselves.

"I could crawl in through the air ducts," Henry said. He was just a little too excited about his first shot at being a field agent.

"This isn't some spy movie, man. And you have to be inside already to even get into air ducts."

"Yeah." Henry sighed. "Maybe we can parachute in. Or climb up the building with some gear. I saw that on TV once."

Amy laughed. "You're looking at this all wrong. We can just walk in through the front door."

Walk in through the front door? This girl was nuts. So I said, "I think they have security here."

Amy shrugged. "And? You just have to look like you're supposed to be there. Blend in, like you belong."

"I saw that in the movies, too," Henry said as he pointed at me. "This guy pretended to be with the power company and got inside anywhere. All you need is a uniform."

"We're kids, Henry," I said.

"You have a better idea?" Amy asked me with a challenging look in her eyes.

"Actually, I do," I said, looking at Henry. "We make a delivery."

They both leaned forward at the same time. "What?" Amy asked.

"Easy." I slapped my hand on my gadget guy's shoulder. "We bring them Henry."

My plan was simple enough: Henry would walk in, pretending to be a CIA employee's kid. While he distracted the guard, we would slip inside. No problem, right?

"So you know what to say, Henry?" I asked as we walked up to the entrance. Amy and I were careful to stay in the shadows.

Henry nodded. He looked a little pale, like he was going to be sick or something. "But . . ." He stopped. "What if they don't believe me?" He swallowed. Tugged at his jacket collar. "They have security, and weapons."

"Relax, Henry," I said, glancing around to make sure nobody was watching. It was starting to get dark in the parking lot, but still. There had to be cameras, right? "Amy and I just have to get to room 355 and grab the book. But we have to keep moving."

"What if they have Tasers and stuff?" Henry was beginning to panic.

Amy pushed him along. "Don't think about all that. Just go with the plan."

"Your mom dropped you off because it's your night to be with Dad," I said, coaching him.

"Right. But . . ." Henry tried to turn back to argue, but Amy pushed him toward the entrance.

"You can do this," I whispered. I was never very good at cheerleading, but I hoped Henry would pull himself together. He looked like my mom did the time Dad and I made her go on Space Mountain at Disney.

I could see Henry's legs shaking as he walked under the glass-cover archway and through the double doors.

"You think he'll be okay?" Amy whispered.

"He looks pretty pale." And then I remembered something Mom did after we went on Space Mountain. You know what I'm talking about, right?

Amy and I didn't have to wait long. The doors were still open as we watched Henry lurch forward, clutching his stomach.

And he puked. All over the fancy CIA seal on the marble floor.

29

AS IT TURNS OUT, PUKING ALL OVER CIA
headquarters' floor is the best distraction ever. Amy and I
hurried inside and slipped past the guards, who were looking confused and grossed out. Henry was still hunched over.
I wondered how many hot dogs he ate in the end. Five? Six?

Amy found the door to a stairwell, and I followed. "Wow,
that was easier than I thought," she said once the door closed
behind us. "I hope Henry's okay."

"He'll be fine. And we're not home free yet." My voice
echoed off the white-painted concrete walls. "We have to
hurry and get that Culper Ring book. John Smith told us 355,
right?"

Amy started up the stairs, taking two steps at a time.

I followed quickly, feeling my backpack bouncing on my back. Once we made it to the third floor, I froze and pointed to the security pad to the right of the door.

We were locked out.

"Now what?" I whispered.

Amy dug inside her pocket. "I kind of figured this might happen. So I borrowed Steve's access card."

"You mean stole, right?"

"Borrowed," Amy said with a smile.

She opened the door, and I followed her into the long hall. I was immediately hit by the smell of antiseptic, like a hospital. There were offices without windows to the outside that lined both sides of the corridor, each with a window that looked out to the hall and door. Some were open. "So where's 355?"

"Let's just look." I hoped we wouldn't run into some CIA guys or ladies. Once you get into a restricted area, you can't exactly claim that you got lost.

We walked the hall, looking inside these boring offices with filing cabinets. Even though the offices were dark, I could see family photos propped on large desks. On the walls, there were calendars and those lame motivational posters in cheap frames.

"It doesn't look very secret in here," I whispered to Amy.

"What did you expect?" she whispered back.

"I don't know. Maybe metal vault doors, one of those pads than scans your handprint. Black walls and supersonic computers and stuff."

"Like in the movies." She snickered, and just then, some guy in a brown suit turned the corner from a hallway to the right we couldn't see. Thankfully, he was busy checking his phone, and we were near an office with an open door.

We ducked inside and hid under a desk. Heard him slowly walk past the doorway. Then he stopped.

Amy and I held our breath.

But then the guy walked on. We both exhaled. I could feel my heart going a gazillion beats a minute.

"Let's hurry," Amy whispered. "We can't afford to get caught here."

I was about to think we might be roaming inside Langley forever when Amy pulled my arm. "There!" She pointed to an office with a 355 plaque next to it.

There was only one problem: A big guy in a blue suit was sitting at a desk right in front of the filing cabinets. He had a small stack of blue folders in front of him.

Amy and I backed up. "This is great." She gritted her teeth. "How on earth are we going to get in there?"

I pulled Amy along and tried the door to another office across the hall. It opened, and we rushed inside.

We found a corner and sat in the darkness. From our spot, we could just see the guy in office 355 through the glass windows. He was twirling his pen as he read something in one of the files.

"You think he can see us?" Amy whispered.

I shook my head. "As long as we keep the lights off, we're fine."

"So how are we going to get him to leave?"

"I'll see if I can't get Henry's help." I borrowed Amy's phone and sent Henry a text.

Have them call the guy in 355

"Let's hope Henry can work his magic," I said. I sat back, watching the guy write something on the paper in front of him.

"This top secret stuff is so exciting." Amy smiled. "When we lived in North Dakota, Mom would let me sit in on the meetings all the time. I'd even get to read her paperwork, stuff she worked on as a governor, whatever."

"And then you moved here." Washington, DC, the city of secrets and locked doors. "Have you thought about telling your mom you miss spending time together? Maybe she could work less or something."

"She's the president of the United States."

"Even a president needs a vacation. And time with her family."

Amy didn't say anything.

I eyed my watch—it had been a couple of minutes since I texted Henry. I had to come up with another plan to get us to the Culper Ring book. "How late do these guys work?"

Amy sighed. "If my mom and her people are any indication, this could take all night."

"Really?" The thought of hanging out in that dark office all night made me itch.

But then I thought of my gadgets. I took off my backpack and unzipped the main compartment.

"What are you doing?"

I smiled as I pulled out a Ruckus on a Roll. "I thought I'd make us some noise."

Amy looked confused.

"Just be ready to run." I moved to the door. Pressed the button on the ball.

And I rolled it as fast as I could.

30

HENRY'S GADGET WAS A SUCCESS—SIRENS were blaring so loud, we had to cover our ears. The noise bounced off the walls of the empty building, making my eardrums pop. This Ruckus on a Roll was awesome!

The guy in 355 got up. He looked confused as he moved to the doorway. Then he covered his ears and rushed down the hall.

We hurried to the office.

Amy was way ahead of me. She ran over to the file cabinet to the far left. Thankfully, the bottom drawer was already unlocked. She crouched down and reached behind the open drawer. Smiled. And pulled loose a small, notebook-size book from the back.

Amy carefully pulled off the strips of silver duct tape. She hesitated and handed it to me. "Since it's your mission."

I tucked it in my coat pocket, and that's when my eyes drifted to the blue files on the desk:

Albert Black

Pandora

I quickly grabbed them and stuffed them under my coat.

Amy was just about to high-five me when the ruckus stopped. The guy had found the ball and turned it off! The dead silence made my ears buzz.

We had to run.

I would like to say my mind was racing, trying to come up with a way to get out of this jam. But it wasn't. My brain just froze, like I was in the middle of a history test.

Luckily, Amy pulled me along. "Let's go!" she whisper-yelled as she stuffed the wads of duct tape in her pocket. But once we peeked around the open door, it was obvious that we weren't going anywhere. The guy was already on his way down the hall. Heading our way, clutching the Ruckus in his palm.

We were trapped.

This was bad. *Really* bad. There was a CIA dude coming our way, and there was no escape.

We both ducked under the desk. But I knew it was only a matter of minutes before the guy would find two stowaway twelve-year-olds.

I heard his feet on the carpet. He stopped in front of the desk. Moved papers around. Banged something down above my head—maybe the Ruckus on a Roll.

"What the . . . ?" CIA Guy mumbled to himself. "Where are my files?"

We were busted. Toast. CIA target practice, no doubt about it.

I closed my eyes and readied myself for a showdown. But the CIA guy turned on his heels. Grabbed something off the desk—the Ruckus. Then I heard him walk down the hall.

The minute the elevator did its little ding, Amy and I crawled out from under the desk.

"Jeez," Amy said, laughing. "I about peed my pants."

I almost did, too, but I wasn't about to admit it. "I think we're about two minutes away from the CIA locking down the whole building. Let's get out of here, huh?"

Henry was still in the lobby, surrounded by grossed-out guards. So when he got a glimpse of Amy and me around the stairway door, he distracted them by pretending to get sick again.

The CIA guy from 355 looked angry, clutching my Ruckus on a Roll in his fist. He was trying to get someone's attention.

Amy and I rushed outside. The cool DC wind actually felt great. We ran to the SUV, where Steve was playing Flying Chickens on his phone. We got in, and Amy made him roll the little divider up.

Henry joined us a minute later. He smiled. "Dude, that was crazy!" His freckles looked like they were going to pop off his face. He buckled his seat belt.

"How'd you get out?" I asked.

Henry shrugged. "I pretended I was going to be sick again and told them my mom was waiting outside. The guards were happy to get rid of me so they could hear about the Ruckus."

"We have to get out of here—*fast*," Amy said, looking worried. She knocked on the divider, and Steve took off. "They have cameras all over the place. Once that guy realizes his files are missing, they'll trace it back to us. And to you, Henry."

Henry swallowed.

And for first daughter Amy, that was really bad news, too. I could just imagine getting grounded at the White House. Maybe they'd make you sit it out in the room in your least favorite color, like the Green Room or whatever.

"Sorry," I said to Amy, like that would help.

But she smiled. "No sweat. I haven't had this much fun since . . . well, forever."

"Me too," Henry said.

"So what's in the book?" Amy asked.

Henry and Amy crowded around me as I pulled the book from my pocket and undid the leather strap. There were drawings—maps, explanations of codes. And pages of numbers with matching names. This book was the key to uncovering the whole Culper Ring.

"Does it say who has the coat?" Henry asked.

"I have no idea," I said, feeling dizzy reading all the codes and numbers. But then I remembered something Andrea said at the International Spy Museum. "George Washington was code name Seven-Eleven, right?"

"That's it!" Amy said.

I carefully flipped the brittle pages until I saw the listing for Agent Seven-Eleven. Next to it, someone had written *Bill Sorenson (George Washington's home)*. "Great, we're back to ol' George again," I said.

"Maybe Bill is at the White House," Henry suggested.

Amy shook her head. "George Washington was the only president to *never* live at the White House. It wasn't built yet."

"So where's his home, then?" Henry asked.

For once, I knew the answer to a history question. It was part of the little bit I'd studied for my history test. "George Washington's home is Mount Vernon."

31

I HOPED THE CIA WOULD BE SLOW TO catch on to our little break-in and borrowing of the files, because Amy had the most to lose. Not only would she wind up grounded in the biggest fortress of America, someone also wanted her dead.

And I worried about Henry—it wouldn't be long before the CIA figured out he was a decoy. Our plan was successful, but maybe it was a bad one anyway.

Since it was already seven o'clock in the evening, we knew we'd have to wait until the next morning to go to Mount Vernon to find Bill Sorenson. Code name Seven-Eleven, the guy with the Dangerous Double.

After Steve drove us back to the Thrifty Suites, I gave Amy the Culper Ring book for safekeeping. We agreed to meet early the next day—with less than twenty-four hours left before the ball, I hoped we'd find the Dangerous Double.

I could tell Henry was working up to ask me something as we walked inside the lobby and I pushed the elevator button.

"You think she thinks I'm dumb?" Henry asked as we got on.

"Who, Amy?" I pushed the number five.

"For not knowing about George Washington not living at the White House and stuff."

And I realized: *He liked Amy.* So I said, "You did save the day, you know. Getting us into the CIA. First daughters must like that sort of thing."

Henry smiled. "Yeah. I did do that, didn't I? That kind of makes me a hero."

"I wouldn't go that far." The elevator doors opened, and we walked toward Henry's room. Don't tell anyone, but it was nice to be roommates. This city was strange, and someone *had* broken into my room. Hanging out with Henry made everything a little less scary.

Still. There was something wrong. It nagged at the back of my brain. And then I realized: I felt naked.

Not naked in the true sense—I mean, that's just gross. But I felt like I was missing something. And then when Henry opened the door to his room, I figured out what it was. My stomach turned.

"Henry."

He turned around and held the door for me. "What?"

"My backpack. I left it at the CIA. All my stuff is in there." I groaned. "The gadgets, my skateboard, my money."

"We can go back," Henry said. I couldn't believe my gadget guy. He was ready to walk out the door to break in all over again.

"What are you going to do: eat another half-a-dozen hot dogs?"

Henry jutted his chin. "If that's what it takes to get the mission done."

And I knew he would, but I also knew it was hopeless. "They probably already found my backpack. Or they will soon enough anyway. We'd only risk getting busted. At least now, we're out of CIA range." I plopped down on my bed and sighed, knowing my backpack was gone. But it was more important to finish the mission. Save the president and Amy. Find the Dangerous Double before this mysterious bad dude would. And before Ben.

Ben. I smiled. "You know, this may not be so bad after all."

Henry gave me a confused look.

"The passport inside my backpack? It's Benjamin Green's."

32

PLACE: HENRY'S MOTEL ROOM

TIME: THURSDAY, 6:00 A.M.

STATUS: GLOATING

HENRY WAS GONE BY THE TIME I WOKE
up, since he was working with Stark and Black to find the
mole. So I took my time getting dressed. The thought of Ben
getting busted by the CIA made me smile.

I mean, I set the guy up without even trying. This was
awesome, right?

But I couldn't enjoy it. The mole had the bomb, and Black
and Stark still hadn't identified him or her yet. I was feeling
the heat. Amy and I were supposed to meet at eight thirty,
to get to Mount Vernon the minute it opened at nine. We
needed that Dangerous Double—as soon as possible. And I

wished I had my backpack.

Henry left me with chalky hot cocoa and a couple of plastic-wrapped pastries for breakfast. I ate them anyway and opened the blue files I'd stolen from the CIA to distract myself from the awful taste.

I started with the Pandora file, since it was the thinnest. Half the forms were mumbo jumbo, but I got some of the reports made by agents.

Unidentified source.

Dead end.

No link to government operations.

It confirmed what I figured out after being followed by all these secret agents: Pandora wasn't CIA at all. So what was it? The CIA didn't seem to know.

Albert Black's file was pretty thick. After half-a-dozen snooze-worthy pages, there was a knock at the door. It couldn't be Henry—he had his own key.

I walked to the door. "Who is it?"

"Agent Stark. Open up." She looked crankier than ever, if that's possible. As she kicked the door closed behind her, Agent Stark pushed something into my chest.

My backpack. The skateboard slammed against my nose, and Dad's compass thumped my arm. I held my backpack and tried to think of what to say.

"You broke into the CIA!?!" Stark gritted her teeth. "I knew you were reckless, but this tops anything I thought you were capable of."

"Thanks," I said before I could think.

That got me the darkest death-ray stare. "That was not a compliment. Did you do this on purpose?"

I shook my head. I wish I'd been smart enough to think of it, though, but I wasn't about to tell Agent Stark that.

She was seriously miffed and started pacing the room. It was kind of scary, so I clutched my backpack like a shield. "What did you take, exactly?"

"I took the Culper Ring book—you know, the new Culper Ring of spies." I told her about our search, leaving out the food fight and our trip to John Smith's campground spot. I figured since Pandora wasn't telling me everything, I could keep a few secrets to myself. "The Dangerous Double is at Mount Vernon," I said, hoping I sounded confident. "I'm going to get it this morning, I promise." I dropped my backpack.

Agent Stark nodded. "Now tell me about the files you stole."

"Huh?"

But Stark didn't buy my fake dumb-kid face.

"Okay, I took a file on Pandora and one on Albert Black."

"Did you read them?" Agent Stark kept her voice low, but it felt like she was yelling the question in my ear.

I didn't see the point in lying, so I nodded. "Pandora isn't CIA at all, is it?"

Agent Stark stepped back. She looked at the door, like someone might come in to save us from our awkward conversation. "No." Stark sat down on Henry's bed, which he'd made, unlike me.

"And you?"

"I was a CIA agent, before I met Albert Black. Deep undercover—I was on the fast track." She laughed, like that was a joke or something. "But then it was all over for me."

"What happened?"

Agent Stark gave me a sad smile, the same kind Dad gives me when something's wrong but he thinks I'm too young to understand. "Long story for another time. But after some department cuts, I was literally carrying my box of stuff out of Langley when Albert Black found me.

"Black told me there was a top secret operation called Pandora," Agent Stark continued. "And he wanted me on it. Pandora had been around for a long time—not that I ever heard of it." Agent Stark shook her head. "I believed him. The work was exciting. And then we got this case at the White House.

"I was beginning to suspect something wasn't right when Sid Ferguson had no idea about Pandora. . . . As the director of National Intelligence he, at least, should know our organization exists." Agent Stark looked up at me. "I need those files. I have to know what I'm part of here."

"Me too. But those pages in there are just mumbo jumbo to me." I handed her the files. Agent Stark went through the Pandora folder first. When she was done, she made a huffing noise Mom makes when she reads my report card. "Just what I thought."

"What?"

"There's an order in here to track the phones of the team. . . ." She looked up at me.

"Already knew that. Ben and I popped the batteries out of ours so they can't track us anymore."

"Good. The mole was probably tracking you that way, too."

It all made sense now: the government, the CIA agents, and the ex-spies—the government and our bad dude mole were all on our tail. I know, I sound like John Smith. But you know I'm right: Everyone really *was* after us.

Agent Stark looked at the file on Albert Black. She flipped back and forth between pages, then closed the folder.

"What does it say?"

"Nothing, really. He was CIA and retired a long time ago." Stark looked bothered, and I knew she wasn't telling me everything.

"What else?"

Stark gave me a sad look. "Trust me, Linc, you're better off not knowing."

33

THURSDAY, 8:00 A.M.

11 HOURS UNTIL THE BOMB

BY THE TIME AGENT STARK GATHERED
the files, I knew two things:

1. Albert Black was a big fat liar.
2. After you use a Sure Shot to sling crab, you shouldn't stick it in your backpack again. Unless you like the smell of fish.

Agent Stark took the two folders and moved to the door. "For now, the CIA doesn't know there are two of you—that there's a Ben Green and a Linc Baker. And we need to guard your double status. Right now, it's Pandora's best secret weapon. But it won't hold up long."

"Where's Ben?"

"We're keeping him hidden so the CIA can't get to him." She sighed. "You got what you wanted, Linc: It's all up to you now."

"I was just trying to get the next clue," I mumbled.

"I hope this lead is worth it." Stark looked me in the eye. "You don't have much time left. Find the coat. Bring it to the White House. If Pandora doesn't crack the case, the CIA will be all over Black. And me." She left, clutching the files.

I took a shower, feeling all stressed out. I could only hope that Culper Ring agent Seven-Eleven—Bill Sorenson—really had the Dangerous Double. Otherwise, our whole mission was a bust, and President Griffin and Amy could die.

No pressure or anything.

I got ready and hurried downstairs to find Amy in the lobby. "Ready to go?"

"Yeah, let's hurry." She looked nervous, scratching at the back of her red wig. "I snuck out, since Steve's catching on."

"How are we getting to Mount Vernon?" I asked.

"I called us a cab." Amy had turned around to walk outside when a dark SUV rolled up. She froze as Steve opened the door and got out. He was seriously miffed and stomped toward the revolving door, where he and Amy ended up twirling around in opposite sections twice before meeting outside.

I could hear the arguing even though I was inside the Thrifty Suites lobby. I wasn't about to join them—I get my share of trouble on my own, thanks.

Steve threatened Amy, telling her he would rat her out to her mom. Amy apologized, and in the end, she got off the hook. Steve made her promise to let him drive us. So he sent the cab on its way and motioned for me to come outside.

We got in the SUV. The second Amy and I were both buckled in, Steve sped away from the motel.

"Gosh, that was a whole new level of intense," I said.

Amy exhaled and let out a nervous laugh. "He's *maaaad*."

"You are making Steve's job very hard." I glanced out the tinted rear window. There was a green minivan, two car lengths behind. For a second, I thought the driver might've been following us. But I couldn't make out a face.

Smith was turning me into a paranoid nut job. I turned back around.

"I hate being the first daughter sometimes." Amy looked really sad for a second but then pulled a map from her pocket. "Anyway. Let's figure out where at Mount Vernon the coat could be." The map showed what looked like a whole town: a mansion, a barn, gardens—the place was huge.

I didn't realize how big Mount Vernon was until now. "Why does it have to be this hard?"

Amy pointed to the map and opened her mouth to say something.

But then my gut told me to look back—and I saw that green minivan, swerving around a sedan to stay close. "We're being followed!"

Amy looked back. "Who?"

"That green minivan." I knocked on the little divider to get Steve's attention.

He lowered the window to the driver's compartment. "What's up, Ben?"

"We're being followed, that's what!"

Steve looked in his side-view mirror.

"The minivan, one car behind us," I snapped. Here I was, a twelve-year-old kid, telling a Secret Service guy how to do his job. This was messed up.

"Buckle up, kids!" Steve called over his shoulder.

I checked my seat belt and grabbed the handle. Amy did the same.

Steve weaved in and out of traffic, then took a sharp right turn, and then another.

"Who's following us?" Amy whispered, like maybe our tail could hear us.

"I don't know," Steve snapped. He was all hyped up, like my friend Daryl gets all the time. He kept looking at his mirrors, then at us, then back to the mirrors. "I think I lost them."

"Are you sure?" I asked. But then I didn't see that minivan anymore.

Steve smiled, like he was realizing he was supposed to make us kids feel better. "Aren't you glad I drove you now, huh?"

"Yeah," Amy said, looking relieved.

I gave Steve two weeks before he'd lose his job. He had to be the worst Secret Service agent ever. And there was something off about him today. He seemed very nervous—like maybe he knew he was about to get canned or something.

"I think we're in the clear now." Steve slowed down and

rolled up the little window. It was suddenly very quiet in our passenger compartment.

Amy picked the map off the floor, and we got back to work.

"So where do we start?" I asked.

Amy pointed at the mansion. "Let's start here and then work our way to the other buildings if we have to."

Steve parked the SUV right near the entrance. There was a banner for Celebrating America's History Week up near the entry—the same as the one I'd taken down at the Smithsonian. The place was bustling with people, and it looked like we were in the 1700s or something. Lots of people in period costume—guys in Revolutionary War uniforms, ladies in poufy dresses.

The big crowd made me nervous. What if we couldn't find this code name Seven-Eleven?

Amy got out of the SUV, and I followed. We hurried to the Mount Vernon entry, because Steve was right about one thing: The clock was ticking. There were just ten hours until the bad dude planned to set off his bomb—I needed to get that coat.

After we bought tickets at the glass booth, Amy and I quickly walked up a redbrick path. We rushed past the welcome center with tall glass windows, down a tree-lined road, and then to the right, between these small white buildings with orange-tiled roofs. We passed a group of African American people in period costume.

"This way," Amy mumbled, poring over the map.

I followed her along a road that looped between the mansion and a giant field in front. Snow caked around the trees, but the field itself was free of snow.

Guys were gathered on the grass, talking, laughing. Looking ridiculous in their 1700s wigs and pants. They were getting ready to have some sort of battle, with rifles at their sides. There was a horse, too, tied to a tree, and about a half-a-dozen cannons lined up.

But then I froze. There was a guy in a blue coat with cream trim, looking a lot like George Washington. "Could that be the Dangerous Double?" I whispered as I pulled Amy's arm.

She looked at the guy. "I don't know."

We walked closer to the group, but as we did, my hope faded. There were no marks from the bullets, and the cream trim looked way too clean and new.

"Not it," Amy and I said at the same time.

"I guess we should try the mansion." I was trying hard not to sound panicked, but I was feeling the pressure. What if Sorenson didn't have the coat? Watching the fake George Washington made me realize how hard it would be to spot the Dangerous Double if there were lots of people wearing replicas at the ball tonight. We had to find it so it would never make it to the event.

Amy pulled out her map. "Let's hope Mr. Sorenson knows we're coming."

"Smith said that the Culper Ring wants to hand over the coat," I said.

We walked past the stables and the washhouse. "Wow,

there's a whole house devoted to laundry? George Washington must've been a messy guy," I joked.

"Hold up." Amy pulled my arm. She pointed at the clothesline behind the washhouse—you could just make it out through the trees. "The Culper Ring used laundry."

"For what?

"To send a message." Amy smiled. "This is Agent Seven-Eleven, telling us where he is."

34

"I TOLD YOU ABOUT THAT WHEN WE WENT
to the International Spy Museum, remember?" Amy said.

"Huh?" I looked where she was pointing. There was an old-fashioned skirt and two handkerchiefs blowing in the wind. "I bet they just did that as part of the whole reenactment day."

"Maybe," Amy mumbled. But she slowly walked closer to the washhouse and studied the clothes that were blowing in the wind. "During the Revolutionary War, one spy would bring information by horse and another would row across the Long Island Sound to bring it to Major Tallmadge. Did you know that they had female spies deliver these messages? Nobody suspected them, because women weren't expected to have a political opinion of their own."

"Amy, I don't have time for a history lesson!"

"Just gimme a minute." Amy pulled the Culper Ring book from her coat pocket. "During the Revolutionary War, the woman spy would let the spy on the horse know in which cove to meet the guy with the boat—and she'd use the laundry on the clothesline to send the message. The code is written in here." She flipped through the book until she got to a page with drawings of laundry on it. "The petticoat tells you he's arrived. . . ."

"So what's it all mean?" I asked, hoping she would focus already.

"There are two handkerchiefs—they're just there to indicate position. And the petticoat is in the third spot, so that means the spy is in the third cove." Amy put the Culper Ring book away and looked at her map. "Only it means something else than a cove."

"What if it's number three on the map?"

Amy and I pored over the map. "The blacksmith shop!" we both yelled at the same time.

Have you ever noticed how hard it is *not* to run when you know you're not supposed to? It would be bad to sprint past the mansion, since everyone would wonder what was up. So we run-walked until you could smell the burning coals and hear the banging of the blacksmith's hammer.

There was a small crowd, gathered to watch the blacksmith work. He was a skinny older guy wearing wire-rimmed glasses and an apron that looked too large on him. The blacksmith had a hot piece of iron between tongs, and he was beating it into shape with a hammer.

"So you think he's our guy?" I asked Amy. We both hung back a little. As much as I would like to think that our code-cracking skills were awesome, I had to admit: We could be totally wrong. And he looked like just a regular dude: kind of scrawny and not spy-like at all.

"Let's just ask him."

"With all these people?" Amy glanced around. There were about a dozen tourists clustered around the blacksmith, and they weren't going anywhere. I guess she had a point.

Thankfully, we didn't have to wait long. The guy finished making some swirly-looking napkin ring, and we all applauded.

"I shall take a break now," he said, wiping his face with a handkerchief. I noticed it was the same type as hung on the clothesline. "More at the hour of one." The dude was really into the whole old-speak thing.

People hung around another minute to look at the horseshoes, napkin rings, and other blacksmith-type stuff that was displayed on the table. But after a short while, we were the only ones left.

"Sir?" Amy called.

The guy turned around. His glasses had drifted down his nose, and he pushed them up. "The show is over now," he said, no longer sounding like he was from the 1700s. "But I'm back at one." He'd already half turned to leave the shop.

But then I said, "Are you Bill Sorenson? Agent Seven-Eleven?"

Bill stopped, turned around, and looked at us both. "They sent kids?"

I smiled. "Least likely to be suspected, just like the original Culper Ring agents during the Revolutionary War."

He liked that. But he looked nervous. "Did you make sure you weren't followed?"

We both nodded. "My driver, Steve, did have to shake a tail, though," Amy the Blabbermouth said.

"So you were followed?" Bill looked like he was about to bolt.

"No, no!" I stepped away from Amy to block his exit. "Just us."

Bill wasn't buying it. "I'll need to see the book."

I nodded and motioned for Amy to show it. Bill took the book and stared at it for so long, I thought my head was going to explode.

"We're on a deadline here," I said. Literally—if we took too long, lives would be lost.

Bill nodded. "I guess this is as good a proof as I'm going to get. Come with me." He motioned for us to come to the back of the blacksmith shop, and we followed him to the door, where there was a duffel bag and a fancy-looking box. Bill picked it up, like there was china in there. It looked just like the hatbox my grandma used to keep her old photos in.

"This is it?" Amy whispered.

Bill nodded. "Best not to open it, considering its powers." He sighed. "I only looked at it once when it was handed down to me by the last Seven-Eleven."

I took the box. It felt heavy, for having just a coat inside.

"We'll make sure the Dangerous Double gets to the president and that it gets stored in a safe place," Amy said.

"Please do." Bill looked sad. I could imagine it was like me giving up Dad's compass. Or harder—I mean, the coat could be used as a weapon.

"How charming," I heard behind me. "Two kid spies and a blacksmith." I turned around and stared at—

"Steve?"

35

THURSDAY, 9:45 A.M.

STEVE LOOKED ALL SWEATY AND AGI-
tated. "I have my own mission to complete." He waved a gun,
motioning for me to hand him the box.

You know I wasn't about to give him the Dangerous Double. But Bill obviously didn't know that, because he grabbed
the box from my hands. "You'll have to get past me first," he
said, clutching the box to his right side. Bill inched his way
past the hot blacksmith oven in the middle of the shop.

He reached behind him with his left hand, grabbing one
of the metal bars. Held it in the fire until it was bright orange.
And he threw it at Steve.

But blacksmithing doesn't make you a good pitcher, it
turns out. Steve just stepped aside and let the hot bar clank
on the shop floor.

"Pathetic." Steve shook his head. Then he pointed his gun toward the ground. And he shot at Bill's feet.

Bill screamed. He let the box slip. It fell to the ground—and as much as Amy and I tried to rush to grab it, it was no use. The lid flew off the top, and the coat fell out of the box like a sad present.

Steve grabbed the coat. "Thank you, Mr. Blacksmith. Or should I call you by your code name—Seven-Eleven?" He smiled. "You're one pitiful George Washington."

Bill looked heartbroken. His feet were fine—Steve had just shot at the ground, not actually at his feet, but Bill was obviously not used to this kind of action.

"You won't get away with this," Amy spat. "My mom will find you."

Steve smiled. "Oh, don't worry. I'll find *her.*" He draped the coat over his arm. Then he turned and sprinted out of the blacksmith shop.

"We have to catch him!" Amy rushed outside.

I followed and saw Steve disappear around the washhouse, where the handkerchiefs were still blowing in the wind.

I looked at the ground, the dirt under my feet. My board was no use here on the loose dirt and caked snow. And they obviously had Secret Service guys train for marathons or something, because Steve was so fast, I'd already lost sight of him.

"He's going to get away!" Amy yelled, running a couple of feet in front of me.

We reached the giant field in front of the mansion, and I felt my stomach drop. There were close to a hundred soldiers, split on two sides, with cannons pointed at each other. Two dudes were on horses right in the middle, with white wigs—one of them was the guy wearing the fake George Washington coat.

"Where's Steve?" Amy asked me, like I could see something she couldn't.

"How am I supposed to know?"

But then I saw him, running behind the crowd of Revolutionary War soldiers. Steve was wearing the Dangerous Double now, so he blended in just enough for no one to take notice.

"There!" I called. I began running toward Steve.

Steve wasted no time pushing his way to the middle of the field. "Off!" he yelled, waving his gun at the George Washington dude on the horse.

The guy slid down the horse and raised his hands. And Steve got on.

Then I saw Henry, sprinting across the field. His face was beet red, his glasses crooked on his nose as he ran as fast as he could. Agent Stark was by his side, looking downright livid.

They figured out Steve was the mole. Stark and Henry hurried toward Steve.

But it didn't matter. Steve was on the horse and looked like he'd been riding all his life. He was probably trained by the Secret Service. The horse resisted, but Steve wasn't taking no for an answer.

Stark came up behind the confused Revolutionary War guys and pulled her gun.

"There's no point," I yelled at her. "He's wearing the coat!"

Steve gripped the reins of the horse and saluted us. "Thank you very much for your help, agents!" He spurred his horse with his heels.

And then he galloped away, like an evil double of George Washington.

36

THE MISSION WAS AN EPIC FAILURE. I
didn't just lose the Dangerous Double—I practically handed
it to Steve. And here I was, so busy trying to stick it to Ben.
Now the presidential family was in even more danger than
before we got here.

I was the worst secret agent ever.

From what Stark told me, Henry figured out Steve was
the mole by matching the opening of the email message at a
White House computer to the location of Steve's Secret Ser-
vice phone or something. Then they tracked Steve to Mount
Vernon. Not that it mattered—we'd all been fooled by him.
And now he had a bomb *and* the Dangerous Double.

Amy looked pale as we found a bench to sit on. "This is . . ." She tried to think of a word but then just shook her head.

"We'll get it back," I said, hoping I sounded like I knew what I was talking about.

The truth? I had no idea what to do now. We'd lost the coat, and it was after ten—making the ball less than nine hours away. Steve would go to the ball, set off the bomb, and get away in the Dangerous Double.

"We'll get it back," I mumbled again.

"No, we won't." Amy sounded like she was about to cry. "I'm really scared, Linc."

I was scrambling to come up with something to say. Some promise or plan to fix it all.

But then I looked up and realized it didn't matter. There was a group of about half-a-dozen guys in dark suits and sunglasses—Secret Service. I felt Amy freeze up next to me. And behind them stood the guy who would put an end to our whole operation.

The director of National Intelligence. Sid Ferguson himself.

We locked eyes for a split second, but then he looked away.

I won't bore you with the details of the drive back. I ended up in a gloomy SUV alone, driven by some Secret Service guy. Amy was going to be grounded "indefinitely"—at least, that's what I heard her mom yell at her on the phone before Secret Service came over and whisked her away. I was pretty sure

President Griffin would get a restraining order against me or something—no more Taco Tuesdays at the White House in my future.

The driver took me to the White House visitor center, where he just stopped like I was on the bus or something. No lowering the window or telling me to get out. Steve was the bad guy, but at least he bothered to make conversation.

At the visitor center, Agent Stark was waiting by the elevator. I expected her to let me have it, but she simply pushed the button to go up.

Stark walked me to the conference room, passing Henry's lab in room 418. I saw there were just a half-a-dozen boxes. Taped up, stacked, ready to go. It wasn't too hard to figure out what that meant.

The mission was a failure. We were all going home.

I followed Agent Stark into the conference room, but I didn't get far. Someone slammed me into the doorjamb. Benjamin Green—but you probably guessed this.

"You grade-A amateur!" He was right in my face.

"Dude, say it, don't spray it." I made a show of wiping my face. To be honest, I was just trying to get away from his bear claw of a grip.

"Agent Green," Agent Stark scolded as she sat at the table. But she didn't get up to help me out or anything.

Ben held on to my shirt a moment longer, giving me a death ray. But he obviously never met my mom. His stare-down was a joke compared to hers, so I wasn't about to back away. "You actually managed to lead the enemy to the objective," he snarled. "That is *beyond* mission failure."

"You didn't exactly perform so great either, showing up after the fact, now did you?" I pushed him away. "At least I found the coat."

"And you handed it to the enemy while putting the first daughter in danger." Ben crossed his arms.

"She chose to join me, you know." I sat down at the table, a few seats away from Stark. "And she's a hundred times the secret agent you are."

Ben practically had smoke coming out of his ears he was so mad. "You set me up to take the fall for your dumb break-in at Langley."

"Oh, that was just a bonus," I blurted out. "See, unlike you, I actually had a mission strategy. What did you think you were going to do with that fake George Washington coat: use your magic wand to turn it into a Dangerous Double?"

"SILENCE!" Albert Black's voice made the conference table shake. And me, too, if I'm honest.

Henry scurried in behind Black and sat next to me. He looked like he was about to cry.

Black slowly walked to the head of the table. He leaned on it and looked at Agent Stark. She looked back at him, and her whole face was a question mark. Black dropped his eyes to his big hands, like he was counting his fingers.

It was so quiet, I was afraid to breathe. Henry sniffled next to me.

Albert Black took a breath. He kept staring at his hands, like maybe they would magically fix everything at the last minute.

Ben shifted, still standing with his arms crossed.

"You all know why I called you here," Black said, his voice deep and tired. "The mission was . . . a stretch from the start." He looked up at each one of us.

Then he slammed the table. Making everyone jump.

Next to me, Henry made a squeaky noise.

"You're all dismissed," Black said, no longer leaning on the table. "The mission was a failure. We're done."

"Permission to speak, sir!" Ben said from his corner of the room.

"There is nothing left to talk about, Green." Albert Black pointed to the door. "Pack up. Go home."

"But the coat is still out there!" Ben yelled. He'd now completely lost his whole super-junior-agent cool. He looked like any other twelve-year-old when an adult put the hammer down. Me, I knew a lost argument when I saw one.

Black walked out in big steps, shoulders stooped. Whatever Pandora was, his operation was a failure. Albert Black looked like a guy who'd just gotten a report card full of Fs.

Ben stomped out, trying to catch up with Black.

Henry sniffled next to me.

"Dude, you can't be crying," I said as I watched Stark get up.

"I'm not," Henry whispered. He exhaled, and I hoped that meant he was pulling himself together.

"Your flight leaves tomorrow at seven," Stark said from the doorway. "The cab will pick us up at five. Don't—"

"Don't be late," I said, finishing her sentence. "I know."

She smiled. "I was going to say, don't feel bad. This

mission was near impossible from the start. You kids just got caught in the crossfire."

Agent Stark's words were still ringing in my ears as Henry and I sat in his room, having chocolate chip cookies and hot cocoa that we snatched from the lobby.

Don't feel bad. Like that was possible.

The cookies were better than the pastries, but I couldn't eat. The mission failure sat in my stomach like cheap birthday cake. I hung out near the window that was painted shut, watching the cars below zoom by. And there was a truck, parked a little ways up the street. Far enough away from the entry not to be spotted but close enough so the driver could keep an eye on things. That driver was John Smith, of course.

He was wasting his time. The case was closed.

I'd called home and got reamed out by Mom for not checking in on Wednesday. Then she asked me if I was eating well and if President Griffin was nice. I lied and told her we had vegetable stir-fry for dinner the night before. She asked about the Junior Presidents Club and that dumb certificate. I lied some more, saying I was getting it tomorrow.

I hung up knowing Mom was happy, but feeling like a total loser myself.

"This is so wrong," Henry said as he stuffed a whole cookie in his mouth. "Wht mbt Aym?"

"What?"

He washed down his cookie with some hot cocoa. "What about Amy?"

I shrugged and walked away from the window.

"This Steve guy is going to wear the coat, isn't he?" Henry took a bite of another cookie, getting more hyper from the sugar. "He's going to take his bomb and go to the ball tonight."

"You don't know that."

But Henry was on a sugar-boosted roll. "Steve is going to take that bomb and set it off. Kill the president, and Amy."

"Henry, calm down."

"I'm not going to calm down!" He tossed his half-eaten cookie on the bed, sending crumbs flying. "This is our fault for not seeing Steve for the evil dude he was."

I couldn't really argue with that. It never occurred to me that Steve behaved so strangely because he was the mole. I wiped the crumbs off my bed. "My flight doesn't leave until tomorrow evening." I checked the clock—it was just after noon. "We have almost seven hours until the ball." *Until Steve would blow up the White House and everyone in it.*

Henry sat back down on his bed. "So what are we going to do?"

I looked around the room for an idea, something to tell my freckly friend. And then my eyes found it.

Ben's box, the one with the George Washington coat in it.

I smiled. "Are you ready to party, Henry?"

37

THURSDAY, 1 P.M.

6 HOURS UNTIL THE BOMB

THE HOT DOG STAND OUTSIDE THE VISITOR
center owed me a frequent customer discount or something, because I went there for lunch again. This time, I was with Ben. It was busy at the vendor, so I left Henry to wait in line while I told Ben about my plan.

We stood near one of the concrete planters, away from other people. I scratched at the knit hat and pushed the glasses up the bridge of my nose. This getup was a real pain, but necessary to keep our double status a secret.

"Let me get this straight," Ben said, glancing over his shoulder to make sure no one could hear. He was wearing a tracksuit and gym shoes, like I caught him in the middle of one of his secret agent workouts. "You want me to disobey orders."

"No," I said slowly, trying to think of a way to sell my plan to him. "Our orders were to save the president and her family, remember?"

Ben crossed his arms. "Albert Black told us to go home."

"And we will!"

Ben punched me in the arm. "Keep your voice down!" He glanced around, but the tourists were all busy eating their hot dogs. Henry watched us from his spot in line—there were four people ahead of him. I was still amazed that his upset stomach at the CIA didn't stop his appetite for hot dogs.

I leaned closer to Ben so he would be sure no one else could hear. "Look, we'll go home like Black said. But that doesn't mean we can't continue our mission and try to save the president and her family."

Ben thought about that. He frowned. "But wasn't the mission canceled?"

"Black said that the mission was a *failure*, but he said nothing about it being over." I was an expert at working within the limits of the rules—even if I was pretty sure I was pushing it. "Why not try to make the mission a success?"

"How do I know this is not just another trap?" Ben asked.

"You don't," I answered honestly. "You'll have to go with your gut—if that's something you even know how to do."

Ben uncrossed his arms. "We both have the same objective."

"Save the president and her family, that's right."

His frown faded, and I knew I had him.

"Imagine if we can get the Dangerous Double," I whispered, watching Henry move up in line. "The mission would be a success, right? And we'll get those medals from the president."

That sealed it for Ben. "Okay, so what's your plan?" he asked.

I forced myself not to smile. "Tonight, at the ball, you go in as part of Amy's protection detail. Just tell Secret Service it was planned that way. Last-minute orders, blah blah."

Ben nodded. "That should work."

"Henry and I will find our way in."

Ben frowned. "Your plan is to sneak inside the White House?"

"We'll all wear costumes, so we blend in," I said. "We need the element of surprise—and we have one."

"Our double status, correct?" Ben asked.

"Exactly. Steve will be looking for the president and Amy, since they're the target. You'll be there to watch out for her. Steve will feel confident knowing where you are—he doesn't know there are two of us."

"Copy that," Ben said.

My plan was to just catch Steve at the ball and stop him—not the best idea, but it was what I had. Like Wilson said: Sometimes, simple is best.

"We can't give up," I said as I saw Henry approach with a tray of hot dogs. "Amy's life depends on it."

Ben nodded. "Agreed. I'll see you tonight, then."

"So you're in?" Henry asked just a little too loudly.

Ben gritted his teeth and got up in Henry's face. "Yes. Now keep it down!"

"Okay, okay," Henry said, taking a spot at a planter's edge. "You want a hot dog?"

"No." Ben gave him a disgusted look. "Do you know what they put in those things?" He went on to tell us—not that it mattered, because Henry just took bigger and bigger bites in defiance.

I couldn't eat. Not because of Ben's speech, but because of what I knew was coming.

I had to catch Steve, the guy with the bomb and the George Washington invincibility coat.

And there were only six hours left.

I ended up watching Henry eat four hot dogs and two bags of chips, washing it down with two sodas. The guy was like a bottomless pit. He threw out his trash and waited for me to join him.

But I saw a familiar truck. Smith—he was parked just up the street.

"I think I'll just stay outside a little while longer," I said from my spot on the edge of the concrete planter outside the visitor center.

Henry shrugged. "Okay. I'll go back to the motel, since my lab space is gone. I'll print out some maps of the White House and work on tracking down those costumes." He left me, letting out a belch as he crossed the street.

I got up from my spot and casually walked over to Smith's truck. Went in on the passenger side. I had to push against Nixon, who seemed to think he deserved the seat more than I did.

"Heard you lost the Dangerous Double," Smith said. He gave me his death-ray glare. "After I practically handed it to you by leading you to the book. The Culper Ring kept that coat safe for over two hundred years!" Some spittle flew in my direction. It landed on Nixon, who put his head down.

I petted the dog, not knowing what to say.

"So what are you going to do to get the Dangerous Double back?" Smith asked, a little calmer now.

"Well, *technically*, we're supposed to just go home," I said.

Smith laughed. "Sounds like you have other ideas already."

I explained my plan, what little of it I had. How we were going to crash the party and catch Steve in the act.

Smith nodded. "Maybe I can help," he said.

"How?"

He smiled. "I'll get you inside the White House."

38

THURSDAY, 6:00 P.M.

1 HOUR UNTIL THE BOMB

WHEN THE WHITE HOUSE THROWS A
party, they don't mess around. We drove by in Smith's
truck—for recon, he said. There were Secret Service guys at
every corner, valets parking cars, dudes in fancy uniform getups, and ladies in giant hoop skirts that barely fit through the
door.

And I was wearing one of those ridiculous getups, too.
The wig made my head itch, and the pants were these baggy
leggings. The only good news: Ben was inside the White
House, wearing the same monkey suit. We managed to rush-
order three kid-size Revolutionary War costumes from the
store where Ben got the George Washington coat replica, and

Henry took a cab ride to pick them up himself. I couldn't wait to get back to my jeans and T-shirt.

"So how are you getting us inside, exactly?" I asked Smith.

Earlier that day in Henry's motel room, Ben, Henry, and I pored over maps of the White House, making sure we knew the layout. But we realized pretty quickly that we simply had to wing it and catch Steve before he could set off his bomb. Ben took off to get inside the White House on his own, while Henry and I found Smith.

"I'll get you inside that white mansion. Be patient, Young Abe," Smith mumbled. We drove past the White House, where we could see the party crowd arriving off in the distance.

I got to sit in front, but that meant I had Nixon on my lap. His tail was smacking against my leg. "I mean, look at all this Secret Service."

"We're not going in through the front door." John Smith drove away from the White House and didn't say anything for a while.

"You have a helicopter, don't you?" Henry said to Smith from his spot in the back. "We'll rappel down in the White House yard or something. Right?"

"*Rappelling?*" John Smith laughed while he parallel-parked in a space that seemed too small for his truck. "Where'd you pick this kid up?" he asked me.

"He's my gadget guy," I said, motioning for Henry to shut up. "He gets most of his spy tactics from the movies." So did I, but I wasn't about to tell Smith that.

"No helicopters." John Smith got out and waved, telling us to follow. He tossed Nixon a couple of biscuits from his pocket and locked the truck. "No need to come in from up high when we can take the low road."

"Huh?" Henry said.

I smiled, because I got what John Smith had planned. "We're taking the tunnel, Henry."

We'd arrived in front of the visitor center. Our outfits got us a few looks from tourists, so we hurried toward the elevator.

"There's a real-life tunnel, going to the White House?" Henry asked as we got on.

"Shhh!" Smith hissed. He glanced around while he used the key around his neck to get us access. "There are cameras and microphones in every elevator."

"Really?" Henry squinted.

We got off the elevator before my gadget guy would get too carried away looking for surveillance equipment.

"I know the tunnels are a great way to crash the party," I whispered to Smith to avoid getting shushed. "But don't we need the keys to get in?"

Smith smiled. "I called in a favor from an old friend."

And that's when I saw Wilson, holding the big metal door open for us. "We have to hurry," he said. "I'm expected at the ball."

Henry, Smith, and I rushed down the tunnel. Henry's jaw was practically dragging on the ground. "Dude, this tunnel is awesome!"

Wilson gave him a hurried smile. "I wish I could give you the proper tour, but unfortunately, we have to run." We did sprint—and it's really hard to run in a Revolutionary War costume, let me tell you. Wilson opened the last few doors, and we rushed up the stairs, where I could already smell some kind of good soup or whatever.

Once we were upstairs, Wilson led us into a small room across from the staff kitchen, where a bunch of chairs were stacked high. "I hope your mission is a success. I wish . . ." He smiled in a sad way.

"You've done enough," Smith said. "Get out of here, before they miss you." They shook hands and hugged, like my dad does with my uncles. And I wondered.

Was Wilson part of the Culper Ring?

I turned to Smith, but he shook his head. "Don't say what you're thinking. Just go up to the East Room. Save the first family."

"Save Amy," Henry said. He looked really nervous.

"We follow the waitstaff inside," I said, trying to focus on my sort-of plan. "Make sure Ben sees us and knows we're there. Then we wait for Steve. Take the coat and stuff." I couldn't get myself to say "bomb." What if we couldn't stop him?

"He's already here," Smith said. "He'll want to take time to blend in. People usually aren't late for a White House gala."

"You think Steve is already at the ball?" Henry asked Smith. He looked stressed to the max. "Right *now*, wearing the Dangerous Double? With a *b-o-m-b*?"

"Chill, Henry." My friend looked like he was about to bolt, and I couldn't have that. I needed him. "Let's go find Steve."

Smith nodded. "I have to run."

"How are you getting out without Wilson?" I asked.

"I'll slip out the staff entrance—this place is hard to get into, but easy enough to leave," Smith said with a grin.

"Wait—how are we going to get back out the tunnels without you or Wilson?" Henry asked Smith.

I glanced at Smith. We both knew that this mission wouldn't go down like that. There would be no quiet escape. We'd either be heroes or get blown to a gazillion pieces. And I couldn't give Henry that last option, because he'd lose his hot dogs all over the fancy White House carpet.

"We'll figure it out, Henry." I pulled him along and opened the door. Lucky us: A slew of waiters was just passing with trays of snacks. "Come on," I whispered. I turned to say bye to Smith, but he was already gone.

Henry and I followed the waiters, careful to hang back far enough not to get noticed. Up the spiral stairs and to the East Room, where the party was hopping. Well, in a grown-up, boring kind of way. On the wall, there was that painting of George Washington. Like we needed reminding of why we were there. The place was crowded, hoopskirts touching, dudes in wigs—they were everywhere.

And to make things worse: I'd already counted a dozen George Washington uniforms.

So which one was the Dangerous Double?

39

THURSDAY, 6:50 P.M.

10 MINUTES UNTIL THE BOMB

I WAS FEELING SICK TO MY STOMACH.
What if I couldn't find Steve in time? I only had ten minutes!

I took a breath to chill out. *Focus.* Our Dangerous Double had marks from the gunfire that George Washington took when he wore it—so I could spot Steve that way, right? But since the coat made you invincible, those marks were really faint. You had to be up close to see them.

I pulled Henry along so we could roam the crowd and find Steve.

Henry groaned next to me. "Man, I can't take this stress. I don't think fieldwork is for me. I'm the gadget man." He sounded like he was about to lose it. "Where are Ben and Amy?"

"They're over there, across the room." I saw Ben Green, scanning the room like the good junior secret agent he was. He stood near Amy and the president. Several Secret Service guys were nearby, dressed in period costume but easy to spot.

"Steve has a real bomb," Henry whispered. "Right now, in this room?"

"Just be quiet for a second, Henry." I needed to think. And I needed these people to leave. That was the only way to spot Steve—by how he behaved. He wouldn't want to leave. "Hey, Henry," I said, leaning close to my friend. "How do we clear the room?"

"Fire alarm?"

I didn't see a red lever nearby, so I shook my head. "I have an idea." I smiled and moved close to the table that had a bunch of snacks and a big punch bowl on it. I took a breath and yelled, "It's a rat!"

The room quieted, but not completely. Not yet.

"I saw a rat, right over there!" I yelled, and pointed under the table. "Everyone get out now!"

My words traveled around the room like fresh gossip in a middle school cafeteria. People moved, and some groups quickly headed toward the exit. This was good. The more people got to safety, the better. The place was emptying out—fast.

And that's when I spotted the guy across the room, just a few dozen feet away from the first family.

Steve.

THURSDAY, 6:55 P.M.

FIVE MINUTES UNTIL THE BOMB

THE MARKS ON HIS COAT WERE FAINT but unmistakable. Steve looked up, and I could tell he was miffed that people were leaving. We locked eyes.

Steve froze. He was about fifty feet away from me. And about the same distance from the president, Amy, and Ben, who were surrounded by Secret Service.

Steve looked back at Ben, who stood half in front of Amy. Then he looked at me, confused by the whole double business.

I had to take advantage of this moment and move. *Now.*

"Get down!" I yelled as I charged Steve. I ran into him like a deranged football player, hoping my desperate plan would work.

And I saw Ben run, too.

Our likeness was confusing Steve enough to make him freeze. He stumbled, and Ben and I managed to take him down.

Henry ran up behind us. He sat down on Steve's legs as I put my boot on Steve's left shoulder. Ben rammed his foot into Steve's right arm. Three other Secret Service dudes rushed the president and Amy out of the room.

And then the last two Secret Service guys were all over us. They pushed us aside and lifted Steve up by his armpits. They took the George Washington coat off, and Ben snatched it. We'd recovered the Dangerous Double.

Henry smiled at me. "That was amazing!"

It *was* amazing. Even if I was a little sore from our pileup.

I was about to high-five Henry. But then I saw what the Secret Service guys pulled from Steve's bag.

The bomb.

The two agents got into a frenzy, trying not to mess with the thing as they placed it on the ground.

"We need to call the bomb squad," Ben said. "Get the professionals in here."

"Great idea," I said, pointing at the red numbers counting down. "You think they can get here in three minutes?"

Suddenly, the room was super-quiet. We all stood frozen, watching the numbers tick down.

3:05

3:04

3:03

I couldn't think! Until I remembered my gadget guy and the reason I brought him to the party. "Henry," I said.

He had his eyes fixed on the timer, looking like he was ready to bolt.

"We need you to dismantle the bomb, buddy."

41

THURSDAY, 6:57 P.M.

THREE MINUTES UNTIL THE BOMB

TWICE A YEAR, MY SCHOOL HAS A FIRE drill. Yours probably has one, too. You're supposed to leave the building in an orderly fashion—like that's ever going to happen at a middle school, right? Our class is usually one of the last ones to make it to the football field, and we're always missing Daryl somehow. If there's ever an actual fire at Lompoc Middle School, we're in real trouble.

Let me tell you, my school could learn something about quick evacuation procedures from the White House. By the time Henry crouched on the floor near the ticking bomb, it was just me, Henry, Ben, and a Secret Service guy who had Steve in a gnarly arm lock. The president and Amy had been taken to a "safe haven" (I figured that was code for anywhere but here). And the party crowd had left the building.

"I got this," Henry said. His nerves seemed to have cooled now that he could work his tech magic.

"Do you know how to dismantle this bomb?" I asked Henry. We were at 2:21 now and counting down. *Fast.*

Henry nodded. "I think so." He pulled a small pocket-knife from his Revolutionary War costume coat and tossed his wig aside. "You're lucky I always carry this." Henry popped out a teeny screwdriver from the knife's center. Then he began unscrewing the plastic top off the gray box that was the bomb.

2:09

Henry carefully lifted the cover. He smiled when he saw the cluster of red, black, and green wires. "This is easy."

Steve laughed. "That's what you think? A ten-year-old kid thinks he can dismantle a bomb designed by one of the best explosives experts in the world."

1:59

"Shut up, Steve," I said. "Nobody asked for your opinion." I put myself in between Steve and Henry so Henry wouldn't have to look at the guy.

"And I'm not ten," Henry muttered as he put his pocket-knife down. "I'm twelve. But a ten-year-old could dismantle this, actually."

1:46. I hoped he was right with all that smack talking.

Henry reached inside the bomb. "Here we go," he whispered. And he pulled the black wires.

We all looked at the clock. Held our breaths. It stopped at 1:37.

I high-fived Henry. "That was awesome!"

Henry got up and smiled. He wiped his forehead. "The geek saves the day," he said. "Maybe I'll make the news or something."

But then something awful happened. The clock did some funky number spin, like it was resetting. And then it stopped.

1:00

"What just happened?" Ben asked Henry.

Henry didn't say anything. His eyes darted to the bomb, watching the numbers change. Then he looked at Steve.

Steve just smiled.

0:51

0:50

The bomb was counting down again.

42

0:49

0:48

This was not good.

"This bomb has a backup inside," I said. "It's counting down again!"

Henry crouched down again. He put his head flat against the floor to look at the bomb. "It's a Babushka," he whispered. "I'd heard of these, but . . ."

"Yeah, it got stolen—didn't Stark or Black tell you?" I asked.

Henry shook his head. "I would've remembered that. Why didn't *you* tell me?"

"I didn't think it mattered," I said, feeling like an idiot. "A bomb's a bomb, right?"

"Wrong," Henry whispered.

"What's the deal with the Ba*biba*—whatever?"

0:44

"You know those Russian nesting dolls? They're called babushkas. This bomb is like that. You take off the cover, dismantle the first bomb. And you think you're done, right?" Henry was sweating. "But then the timer resets, because there's another one inside."

"Are you capable of dismantling it?" Ben asked. He looked seriously stressed, too.

Henry nodded. "I can, but the clock will just reset for the next bomb, hidden inside this one. It's pointless."

"So it's worse than a double," I mumbled.

0:32

Ben turned and pulled Steve toward him by his shirt collar. "How do we dismantle this explosive device? Answer me!"

Steve looked pretty scared—Ben was impressive that way, even if he was just a twelve-year-old kid. But everyone (including Steve) knew Steve had the upper hand. "You can't dismantle it," he said. "It's designed to blow. No matter what."

0:18

"Henry, you need to scram while you can," I said.

"No." He shook his head, but you could tell that he was thinking about leaving. Let's face it: I wanted to make a run for it, too. "There's not enough time to get out of the blast zone anyway," Henry said. He was right.

0:14

We were going to die in the East Room of the White House. And all I could think about was my family. How I wanted them to be proud of me for belonging to the Junior Presidents Club, even if it was all a lie. And how I'd never get to ride my skateboard to Daryl's again. Or beat Sam at Racing Mania Nine when it came out next month.

0:11

Pull yourself together, Linc!

Steve smiled at me.

"At least Steve here is blowing himself sky-high right along with us," I said. "So much for the invincibility coat." And then I realized: the answer to solving this crisis was right under my nose.

"Ben! Give me the coat!" I reached out.

0:07

Ben had the Dangerous Double draped over his arm. "Why?"

The guy was going to question me now, with five seconds left on the clock?

"Just give it!" I yelled.

Ben tossed me the coat.

I held the Dangerous Double by the shoulders, draping it in front of me like I was helping someone put on the coat. Then I dropped my whole body on the bomb. I saw the numbers on the timer flash before they disappeared under the fabric.

0:02

I wrapped the coat around the bomb like it was a present. Tucking the corners all neat and tight, just like Mom taught me.

I closed my eyes. Gritted my teeth as I cupped myself around the bundle.

And felt the bomb explode against my chest.

43

THURSDAY, 7 P.M.

HAVE YOU EVER BANGED YOUR ELBOW
really hard, right on the funny bone? The explosion felt like
that, only it went through my whole body. My ears were ringing. My vision blurred. I think I screamed, or someone did
anyway.

But it worked. Wrapping the bomb in George Washington's invincibility coat was not how I'd pictured things would
go down, but then, the best stuff happens when you tear up
the plan anyway.

I was curled up in a ball on the floor, clutching the coat
and bomb. Eventually, Henry pulled my arms away. Ben took
the bundle and slowly unwrapped the Dangerous Double.

What had been the bomb was now a melted mess of
metal, wire, and scorched parts we couldn't recognize. The

Secret Service guy called in for backup. Ben carefully placed the bundle of bomb parts in a corner and then took off to keep our double secret.

I tried to get up, but my legs were shaking too badly.

Henry sat down next to me. "Dude, you just saved the White House."

"You think I'll get extra credit?" I joked, my voice croaking.

Henry laughed. "You should."

I sat up, watching the room spin. The place smelled like burnt plastic.

"Amy is okay—we saved her," Henry whispered.

I didn't say anything, mostly because my jaw hurt too much to talk.

Henry smiled. "Maybe I'll ask her out for hot dogs."

Steve was arrested, and the Dangerous Double was taken away by Albert Black. Apparently, the mission was back on after all.

Our botched gala even made it on TV—"Rats at the White House" ran on all the networks as breaking news. Not that the White House was giving them much to go on. The news guys interviewed one guest who talked about some kid who saw a rat, but that was all the actual evidence there was.

Of course, there was the in-depth report on the health dangers of rat droppings, including a daylong shadowing of an exterminator. Then a special on the history of rats—and what might happen if the plague came back. The news dudes interviewed a doctor for three hours about the dangers of vermin droppings in food (yuck) and blah blah.

No talk about the plot to kill the president and her family. And not a peep about the George Washington invincibility coat. Henry would examine the coat in his lab before it was stored in a safe place. No word on where that was.

The mission was a success.

So why did I feel like something wasn't finished?

44

PLACE: THE WHITE HOUSE KITCHEN

TIME: FRIDAY, 8 A.M.

STATUS: HUNGRY

THE NEXT MORNING, WE WERE ALL invited for breakfast with the president herself. Amy met Henry and me in front of the White House. She gave Henry a quick tour of the state floor, just like she'd shown me on Taco Tuesday.

"So you're not grounded anymore?" I asked her as we walked upstairs to their private quarters and toward the kitchen.

"Oh, I still am," Amy said. "Mom made me promise not to sneak out or borrow anything without asking. Especially her files." She grinned. "She did say she'd let me hang around the office sometimes. Oh, and we're taking a vacation!"

"Where are you going?" Henry asked her.

"Top secret." Amy leaned closer. "But it may or may not be Italy. Mom has to wrap up some stuff, but then we're going—and Dad's meeting us there."

We sat down at the kitchen table with the whole Pandora crew and President Griffin. There were crepes, eggs, bacon, and fresh rolls—nothing like the plastic-wrapped stomach bombs we ate at the motel. Everyone was rehashing the case, talking about how close Steve came to blowing up the White House.

Me, I had a hard time feeling relaxed. Washington, DC, made me feel paranoid. Who could I trust? Why was Wilson, a Culper Ring agent, in the White House—and what was up with Pandora? Maybe I'd been hanging around John Smith too long.

"What made you jump on the bomb, Linc?" President Griffin asked while I loaded a second plate.

I had no idea. It was a crazy thing to do, but it made sense at the time, like most of the stuff I do. "I don't know. I guess I figured that if the coat made the person inside it invincible, it might keep us safe from the explosion."

"Quick thinking," President Griffin praised. And then she checked her watch. "Unfortunately, I really must go now." She looked around the room at Ben, Stark, Black, Henry, Amy, and me. "It's been a pleasure. Mr. Black, I'm sure we'll talk soon."

He nodded. I wondered what that was about. But only for a second—there was a pile of bacon with my name on it.

President Griffin left, and Amy followed to go call her dad, she said.

Albert Black stood, like he was ready to make a speech. "Well, I'm sure you've all heard by now that Steve has been questioned. Looks like he had some sort of political agenda and decided to act on it when he heard about the coat."

"Then he was a lone operative," Ben said. His plate was clean, like it never had food on it at all. "There are no organizational ties or intel on continued operational movements."

"What's he saying?" I whispered to Henry.

"That Steve worked alone," Henry answered.

"Oh." I chewed on my bacon. It made no sense, though. "But how did he even know about the coat?"

Black shrugged. "Intel. He was Secret Service."

I thought about Steve and how he rode away on that horse at Mount Vernon with such ease. "So Steve is Mustang, you know, in the email. But then who is Dagger?"

"Whoever he is, he covered his trail," Stark said. "We're leaving the hunt for Dagger with Secret Service. With the Dangerous Double recovered and the bomb threat neutralized, our mission is complete."

"Right," I mumbled. Suddenly, I wasn't hungry anymore. I watched Black and Stark take off, talking in whispers.

Ben got up, too. Then he surprised me and extended his hand. I shook it. He nearly broke my fingers. "You were vital to this mission's success. I believe you won our bet. The Presidential Medals of Freedom will be handed out this afternoon, and I'll give you mine."

"Thanks. But I couldn't have done it without your help, taking down Steve and all," I said, hating to admit it. "So I guess we both won, sort of."

"Fair enough. I'll be gathering my belongings," Ben said as he left the table. "All best to you both on your future assignments." Then he smiled. "Disregard. You're a civilian, so you'll be going home, Baker."

For once, Ben was right: It was time to go home. And after that bomb turned me into a human blender, I was happy to leave Washington, DC, and all its secrets and spies to the professionals. This place was too much for a California kid like me. I even missed the Lompoc fog.

Henry wanted to talk to Amy, so I ended up going back to the motel by myself. I didn't mind. Since my flight wasn't until seven that evening, I had some time to kill. My head still kind of hurt, and I was hoping to get a nap in.

But then something weird happened. The lady at the motel desk called for me. "Young man!"

I walked up to the counter.

"A message came for you early this morning." The lady smiled and dug under the counter for a white envelope with my name on it. "Here you go."

I took it and sat down on the super-uncomfortable couch in the lobby.

For Sale: 1984 Lincoln
This beauty has more than meets the eye
$1,000. Last chance!

I checked the clock in the lobby. It was almost ten o'clock. Smith's favorite meeting time.

FRIDAY, 10:05 A.M.

AS IT TURNS OUT, I'M AN EVEN FASTER skateboarder than I thought. I managed to make it to the Lincoln Memorial just five minutes after ten.

I took my board. Sat on the steps for a minute to catch my breath. I watched as a bunch of guys and ladies were roping off an area in front of the Lincoln Memorial for the president's speech. In the middle, there was a low podium about the size of my living room. I didn't spot Smith, only more guys who were setting up speakers.

I walked up to the giant Lincoln statue, where I hoped my spy guy might find me like before. But I didn't see him. All I spotted was that same banner for Celebrating America's History Week, with George Washington staring me down.

I let the bright sun warm me up as I walked back down the stairs of the Lincoln Memorial.

"Watch out!" someone yelled.

I looked down and realized I'd just stumbled on John Smith. He was sitting on the steps with Nixon at his side. The dog licked my hand when I petted him. How had I missed him?

"I got your message," I said as I sat down.

"Can't stay in one spot too long, Young Abe."

"I know, the agents," I said. I didn't see anyone who looked suspicious, but I figured I wouldn't argue with him. And for all I knew, some of the staff setting up for the celebrations were agents.

John Smith grunted. Waved his hand in dismissal. "Not much time."

"Your message . . ." I said.

"Shouldn't have even sent it," Smith said. "They're still watching."

"Here?"

"Not yet." Smith fed a treat to Nixon. "But you being late doesn't help."

I waited for him to get to it already. From dealing with Grandpa, I knew that sometimes you had to let a cranky person get their bad mood out before they started to make any sense.

"We caught the bad guy, you know. Couldn't have done it without your help getting us in the White House," I added, hoping to butter him up. "So thanks."

Smith nodded. "I heard they're going with the lone gunman theory."

"Yeah. He's just some nutcase who hated the president."

"If you believe that, you're even dumber than you look."

"Thanks for the compliment." I added, "But I did wonder who that Dagger person is. You know, the one who sent the messages."

Smith stared off in the distance and kept petting a happy Nixon. Some ladies were pinning red, white, and blue ribbons along the podium. "Information is a powerful thing. Truth, even more so. 'Truth will ultimately prevail where there is pains taken to bring it to light.'"

"Huh?"

"It's something George Washington said." Smith shook his head. "Never mind. The point is, Young Abe, that the truth is also easily manipulated."

"Like on the news." All those reporters chasing the rat story like it was the end of the world. One dude even had his cameraman take a close-up of rat poop. Talk about disgusting.

Smith leaned closer. He smelled of cinnamon and sweat— not a good combo. "Or in intelligence reports."

"What do you mean?" I asked, ignoring the stink. "Stop talking in code already, and just tell me why you wanted to meet me here."

"Did you ever wonder how your criminal secret agent Steve got his intel on the coat?"

I shrugged. "From the president? Secret Service guys hear everything all the time."

"And how did President Griffin know the attack was coming?"

"Intelligence," I said, trying hard to remember how the whole crazy mission got started. I remembered talking to Stark, when she came to California to find me for the mission. "There was an email. Dagger was planning to steal the George Washington invincibility coat and use it to kill the president at her fancy ball."

"And where did this report with the email come from?" Smith asked, sounding like a kindergarten teacher.

I tried to think back to when Stark first told me about the threat on Sunday, when she was waiting for me down the street from Sam's. "The Daily Brief or something. Isn't that from the CIA and stuff?"

"The Presidential Daily Brief." Smith nodded. "But if Steve only followed you kids to find the coat, why was the plan to use the coat to kill the president already reported?"

I took a breath. Smith was right: It made no sense for Steve to have been the one and only guy. "He never seemed smart enough anyway."

"Thinking with your gut, Young Abe. Now you're talking." Smith touched his nose, telling me I was right.

Some guy was testing the sound system. Piercing noise bounced off the stone, then silence.

"So who came up with the plan?" I asked.

"Who delivers the Presidential Daily Brief?" Smith fired back.

I opened my mouth, but Smith covered it with his palm.

His hand smelled like dog biscuits.

"Don't say his name." Smith glanced around. "You never know who's recording this." He got up and wiped the dog hair off his pants, making it fly in my face.

"Now what am I supposed to do?"

"You'll think of something." Smith walked away with Nixon trailing him, hoping for another biscuit.

This was just great. I'd diffused a bomb, and it still wasn't enough. Now I had to take down the big bad dude.

The guy who called himself Dagger.

Sid Ferguson.

46

JUST IN CASE YOU THINK I'M SOME SORT of hero after that whole bomb situation, I should tell you that you're wrong. I'm just Linc from California, that twelve-year-old kid who gets into trouble. A lot. Linc, who barely gets passing grades in school but can kick your butt at Racing Mania Eight.

Not Linc the junior secret agent who takes down the director of National Intelligence. I was beginning to think I might've given people the wrong impression by hugging that bomb.

But now I had a problem. I knew the truth about this plot to kill the president. The real bad guy wasn't Steve—it was Sid Ferguson. And he was still roaming around the president, doing whatever it was that the director of National Security did, only in an evil kind of way.

So maybe Pandora had saved the president. *This* time. But for all I knew, Ferguson was planning his next assassination attempt right now.

While I was here looking at the giant statue of Lincoln, someone suddenly came up next to me. "Penny for your thoughts." Amy snickered, making me jump. "Get it? Lincoln's on the penny."

"Clever joke. Give me a minute to contain myself."

"Jeez, who ate your homework?"

"Sorry." I sighed. "How did you even find me here?"

"I wanted to say good-bye before you left, so I called the motel," Amy said. "Mom told me it was okay. So anyway, the motel lady told me you got some weird message about a car, so I figured you were here."

I spotted a new Secret Service lady a dozen feet away— earpiece, dark suit, brown hair in a bun. She was hard to miss. She had her back toward us and was scanning the area. Watching the crews set up for the celebration. "New babysitter?"

"She's okay. Today is the last day of the Celebrating America's History Week—did you see it out there?"

I nodded. But I couldn't care less.

"There will be dancing, and Mom is doing a speech—"

"That's great," I snapped.

Amy blinked.

"Sorry," I said, realizing how I sounded.

Amy pointed to the stairs. "Let's get away from the people, and you can tell me what's up."

We found a quiet spot, away from the setup crew and the podium. I told her about Ferguson and how he planted the intel in the Presidential Daily Brief. How he was Dagger, the real bad guy behind the bombing.

"He used Mom. Ferguson knew she'd bring Pandora in to find the coat. So all his slimy guy Steve had to do was wait for you to find the Dangerous Double so he could steal it. And Ferguson didn't have to get his hands dirty—plausible deniability." Amy was fuming.

"Ferguson is an expert liar," I said.

"And we have no proof." Amy sighed.

"No." But then I had an idea. It wasn't the best I ever had, but then, this was crunch time. "So we get the proof. A confession."

"How?" Amy looked at me with sad eyes.

"A guy like Ferguson won't show up unless you've got something he wants."

Amy frowned. "We don't have anything."

"Actually, we do. We have the Culper Ring book," I said.

Amy looked shocked. "You can't be serious. We can't give him that. He'll know the identities of all the Culper Ring spies. We should burn it," Amy whispered.

"No," I said. "I'll find a safe place for it. But first, I want to take out Ferguson."

"By luring him with the Culper Ring book?" Amy shook her head. "No. It's too risky."

"Haven't you learned from these CIA dudes? We don't give him the real book." I gave her my best Linc smile. "We give him a double."

47

FRIDAY, 11:45 A.M.

DON'T TELL ANYONE THIS, BUT I ONCE
forged my mom's signature when I got an F in math. Not that
it really worked—Mom found out in the end when my report
card went out, and I had to fess up. But the forgery was never
discovered.

My skills came in handy when we worked on the Culper
Ring book. I mean, it had to look authentic enough if we were
going to fool Sid Ferguson, right? I used the real book to fake
some of the code systems that the spy ring used—like the
whole laundry business—but messed up enough to make the
information useless. Now I was copying numbers with names
from the phone book we borrowed from the Thrifty Suites
reception desk.

"You really think he's going to buy this?" Amy kept looking over my shoulder, then pacing Henry's motel room. She'd bought the leather-bound book for us. We'd soaked the pages in watered-down coffee from the lobby and blasted it with the blow-dryer to make it seem old—thankfully, Ferguson didn't know what the real Culper Ring book looked like. Or I hoped he didn't anyway.

"It'll work," Henry mumbled. He was chewing on his cuticles.

"Quit stressing me out, guys. You're not helping." I hated being the calm one. I wrote down another series of numbers—467—and copied a name from the phone book. "Let me focus."

Henry obviously didn't hear me, because he kept asking me about my plan. "So how is this going to work? I'll be recording the conversation, right?"

"With your camera, yes. I can't do it, because Ferguson will be looking for a wire on me." I'd seen enough crime shows with Grandpa to know how this worked. "All you have to do is be nearby." I wrote down another number with a made-up spy name.

"How close do I have to be, exactly?" Henry asked. His voice sounded like someone was giving him a wedgie.

"I don't know, Henry. Close enough to catch him with the camera."

Henry was very quiet. It wasn't until I was done making my fake Culper Ring book that he spoke up. "I can't do it," Henry whispered.

"What do you mean?" I sounded pretty snippy, but let's face it: We were running out of time.

"I can't be out in the field like that. Not anymore." Henry's face was pale, and his eyes were panicky. "After that bomb situation, I just . . . I'm not brave like you."

I could tell he was majorly stressed out. And Henry was the gadget guy, not a field agent.

"I'm sorry, man," he whispered.

"Don't be." I gave Henry a punch in the arm. "You did your time as a field agent—first at the CIA, then at the White House."

"We couldn't have caught Steve without you," Amy said.

"See? You already saved the first daughter," I said.

Henry smiled. "If you're sure. But who are you going to get for the video?"

I looked at Amy. She looked at me. We both knew: It was down to the two of us now.

Amy went out to check in with her new Secret Service lady— she was waiting for Amy in the lobby.

I should have walked her downstairs. But I was too busy sweating like crazy, since it was just about time to call Ferguson. I dug the card he gave me on Taco Tuesday from my pocket and used the phone in Henry's room while Henry was checking the camera again.

What if Ferguson didn't fall for my story?

I didn't have to worry. I pretended to be Ben on the phone,

and he took the bait instantly. It was so easy—a little *too* easy.

"But why wait until three to meet?" Ferguson said.

Because that's how long we need to set up our plan. I couldn't tell Ferguson that, so I fired back, "Why not?"

I could hear Ferguson laugh.

"What's so funny?"

"You and your scheme. What are you doing up there—making a fake Culper Ring book?"

How did he know that? And what did he mean by "up there"?

"Your little friend Amy told me everything," Ferguson went on. "She's quite the talker if you threaten her family."

"You have Amy?" I muttered. I felt the blood drain from my face.

"Caught her right in the lobby of your motel. Or my new Secret Service agent did—you'll remember her from the little break-in you had earlier this week?"

I tried to say something, but my mouth was too dry to talk.

"I find it's good to have leverage." Ferguson paused. "Let's meet someplace public. How about— "

"The Lincoln Memorial," I said quickly. I needed it to be somewhere familiar.

Ferguson hesitated. "Why not? This is my city after all—and the place is already crawling with my agents. But we'll meet at one thirty. Oh, and Ben?"

"Yeah?" I said.

"Let's make it just you, me, and Amy, shall we? If I see

even one of your sad Pandora team members, Amy is dead. You understand?"

"Yes."

"I'm so glad we understand each other. You really do make a great agent, Benjamin Green."

48

FRIDAY, 12:47 P.M.

I JUST SAT THERE ON THE BED IN HENRY'S motel room, holding the phone. Ferguson's words were still ringing in my ear.

If I see even one of your sad Pandora team members, Amy is dead.

"Linc?" Henry gently poked me in the shoulder.

I looked up at my friend. "He has Amy." I told him about the rest of the conversation.

Henry sat next to me. "So I can't come with you now, not even if I wanted to."

I shook my head. "Ferguson said he'll kill Amy if he sees any Pandora members." But as I said the words, I thought of one Pandora member who could help me. One guy who could show up at the Lincoln Memorial and get past Ferguson's men.

"I have an idea!" Henry jumped up as he thought of the same person I did. The guy I hated most.

Benjamin Green.

I left Henry and Ben a few blocks away as they went over the plan one last time. It was a pretty simple operation, but it involved some tech, so Henry had to explain it to Ben about a dozen times.

Me, I was practically shaking as I rode my skateboard to the Lincoln Memorial. Ben would be right behind me. Because we looked alike, we counted on him being able to slip past Ferguson's men and execute our plan. Without Ben, the whole thing would be a bust.

By the time I made it to the Lincoln Memorial, I had a single focus:

Save Amy.

Even if it meant giving up the real Culper Ring book. I couldn't risk trying to pass off the fake, especially since Ferguson already knew about our plan. The place was bustling with tourists, secret agents, and people in period costumes. The stage was all put together now. There was some old music playing over the speaker system, stuff that sounded like it was from the 1800s or something.

I made my way up the steps and looked up at the white columns of the Lincoln Memorial. I was about to meet with the director of National Intelligence, the guy who wanted the presidential family dead and held Amy hostage.

What if our plan didn't work?

I was freaking out. *Big time.* So I took a breath. It was one twenty-nine, one minute before our meet time. The place was packed. And I had no way to tell who were the good guy agents and who were the evil ones on Ferguson's team.

I popped the battery back into my phone. Dialed Ben's number and muted it. I stuffed it in my pocket, along with my last Ruckus on a Roll.

"Benjamin Green," I heard next to me. Sid Ferguson was like a ninja, I swear.

"Hi," I said, hearing my voice skip.

Ferguson got really close to me. "Open your coat."

I did. I even lifted up my black sweatshirt—Ferguson was making sure I wasn't wearing a wire. "See? No recording equipment." I sat down.

"Your cell phone," he said, extending his hand.

I gave him Henry's, following our plan.

Ferguson dropped the cell phone on the ground and crushed it with his foot, grinding the plastic into bits with his heel. So far, he acted as I expected. I only hoped my call to Ben had gone through.

Ferguson sat to the left of me on the Lincoln Memorial steps. "You have what I need?"

"I do," I said, feeling the weight of the Culper Ring book in my left pocket. "But first, I want you to tell me what you're going to do with it."

Ferguson was silent for what seemed like forever. We

both looked out on the Reflecting Pool, which stretched in front of us, the Washington Monument standing straight and tall off in the distance. The crowd below, waiting to see the performance onstage.

"The George Washington coat," I said, prodding the guy, hoping he didn't hear how nervous I was. I pulled my phone from my right pocket and slid it down my side to place it on the stone step, tucking it next to my leg where Ferguson couldn't see. "How did you even know about the Dangerous Double?"

Ferguson leaned his hands on his knees and sighed. "Albert Black and I were partners in the CIA; did he tell you that?"

I shook my head.

"We served in Russia during the Cold War. Things got heated. . . ." Ferguson paused, and his face went dark, like he was remembering something bad. "Albert went on to do some black ops, while I moved up the ladder." He motioned around, like he built Washington, DC, or something. "So a few months ago, I hear rumors about Pandora, a black ops team out to find mysterious artifacts."

"Dangerous Doubles," I said. I glanced at my phone. The call was still connected. But the plan was not in motion yet.

What was keeping Ben? I searched the crowd and thought I spotted him behind some ladies in hoopskirts.

"Dangerous Doubles—that's right. We had a file on the Culper Ring, but there wasn't much progress for decades. Until I heard this story from a friend who works black ops, something about a George Washington coat that made you invincible." Ferguson smiled. "It was easy after that. All I had to do was bring Pandora here to find the coat for me."

"That lady who stole my file at the airport. You had her and that bald dude break into my room?"

"I needed to make sure I got the Dangerous Double, Ben. And that meant keeping a close eye on you and Pandora." Ferguson shook his head. "They were a little messy about the break-in—I apologize for that. Sloppy work. You weren't supposed to know they were there."

"It was kind of hard to miss the mess." I tried not to get angry—I had to focus on getting Amy back. Catch Ferguson in his lies.

"The book—now that was just gravy," Ferguson mused. "Dozens of names revealed. The whole Culper Ring exposed."

I heard a piercing sound over the speaker system down below. "Where's Amy?" I asked.

All of a sudden, Ferguson got really close, like a snake going for its prey. "First, *where's my book?*"

I swallowed. Glanced around the Lincoln Memorial, relieved to find some familiar faces. That African American couple, pretending to study a map. The German tourists, taking pictures of the Lincoln Memorial while also snapping shots of us. *They had traced my phone signal.*

And there was Ben, at the sound station. Hooking up his phone with one of Henry's cables like we'd planned.

But I also saw the lady who'd stolen my file at the airport—Amy's new Secret Service agent—and her bald guy sidekick, who'd helped her toss my motel room. I had backup, but so did Ferguson. And something told me he wouldn't go down as easy as Steve.

"First, I want an answer. Why kill the president?"

Ferguson tossed me a death-ray stare. "This woman thought she could change the way the intelligence community does business. She was going to make me open all my files—that simply couldn't happen."

I heard a soft thud over the speaker system, followed by a quick squeak. And I knew it was now or never.

"So you tried to have Steve blow her up," I said.

Ferguson checked his watch. "She has a speech in about an hour." Then he smiled and said, "I'll kill President Griffin today."

Kill. Kill.

President Griffin.

The words echoed around the Lincoln Memorial over the speaker system.

Exposing Ferguson as Dagger.

FRIDAY, 1:41 P.M.

I SAW THE AGENTS' EYES SCAN THE AREA until all homed in on me and Ferguson on the steps. The guy was busted.

And he knew it. Ferguson jumped up but then stood frozen.

I pointed toward Ben. "See that guy? He's the real Benjamin Green."

Ben saw me look and gave me a nod.

"All those agents out there? They know you're the real bad guy now."

Ferguson went pale. His eyes were darting frantically.

"Where is Amy?" I hissed. Then I spotted them in the crowd: the two guys, the dude in the sports coat and the

muscular guy, the ones who had trapped Ben at the Smithsonian. Amy was wedged between them. They were about twenty feet away.

Thankfully, Ben and the government agents—my backup crew—saw her, too. But they were on the other side of the plaza—I had to get her away from those bad dudes!

So I jumped up, clutching my phone. Yelled over the speaker system, "Amy!"

She looked terrified. I knew our good-guy agents could get Ferguson's bad dudes, if only Amy was out of range.

"Your shoes!" I yelled, hoping she understood. I turned on the Ruckus on a Roll and held it near my phone, hoping to distract Ferguson's men. Noise bounced off the stone, surrounding us all with the blare of sirens.

Amy gave me a confused glance and looked down at her shoes. But then I saw that she knew what to do.

"Double knots!" I hollered over the ruckus. "Get down!"

And Amy dropped to the ground.

50

ADVICE FOR ALL THE BAD GUYS OUT
there: don't mess with the Secret Service. Or the CIA—they
were all over Ferguson's bad dudes and had them in cuffs
within seconds.

Amy was flat on the ground. When she saw it was safe,
she got up. Stark whisked her to safety. I turned off the Ruckus
on a Roll.

Ferguson didn't even try to make a run for it. The CIA
agents cuffed him and took him away.

Ben was telling the Secret Service agents what happened.
This was his territory. And I was happy to leave the secret
agent stuff to him again. Our double status sure made for a
great secret weapon—a secret I was glad to keep by scram-
ming.

As I snuck away from the Lincoln Memorial, I was jumped by Nixon. That crazy spy Smith was here somewhere. I needed to talk to him, before he drove off into the sunset with that silver trailer.

It didn't take me long to spot him. Smith had his truck and trailer parked behind the Lincoln Memorial, in the same spot as when we first met.

Smith gave me a nod. "Nice work." He petted Nixon. "You did okay, for an amateur kid agent."

"Yeah, well. I had some help from an old guy." You could do worse than having Smith in your corner.

That got me a laugh.

"Can I ask you something?"

Smith shrugged.

"Are you part of the Culper Ring?"

Smith shook his head. "I'm not part of anything, haven't been for a long time." He hesitated. "I just hid the book at Langley, that's all."

"Pretty smart."

"It was only meant as a temporary hiding place," Smith said. "I knew someone would find it if they went looking. Anyway, I'll be off here in a sec. Anytime now, they'll come and erase the witnesses' memory."

I would like to say he was nuts, but after what I'd been through the past few days, I was pretty sure John Smith might be the smartest guy in Washington. And I needed his help with one last thing. "Will you hide this again?" I dug into my pocket and pulled out the Culper Ring book. The real one.

Smith took it. "You're giving this to me?"

"I don't know who else to trust."

Smith nodded. He tucked it into the pocket of his faded army jacket. "I'll guard it."

"One last question."

"Don't bother, Young Abe," Smith said quickly.

"You don't even know what I was going to ask," I said.

Smith got close enough so he could whisper. Not that anyone was listening in. "You want to know if there are more of those—Dangerous Doubles you call 'em, right?"

"Right. And Wilson is part of the Culper Ring. But how about Albert Black?" I'd checked the book, but his name wasn't in it.

Smith gave me a smile and moved toward his truck. "You're gonna have to ask Black yourself." He got into his truck and started the engine. "Good luck, Linc," he called from the window. "It's up to you kids now to change things."

So after I left Smith at the Lincoln Memorial, we all had pizza at the White House. It was a classic happy ending, what can I say?

Well, *almost* a perfect ending anyway.

"How is President Griffin going to explain Sid Ferguson's crimes?" Henry asked Albert Black.

Black smiled. "They'll have him do up some phony statement about retiring to spend more time with his family. And then they'll interrogate him to find out how deep this conspiracy goes."

"You're not telling people that Ferguson tried to kill the president? Not even after the whole scene at the Lincoln Memorial?" I couldn't believe it.

"They'll just pretend it was an exercise, or they'll make up some other story to cover it up."

"Like 'Rats at the White House,'" I said.

"Exactly. Think about it, kid," Black said, leaning on the table with his heft, making his plate slide against his stomach. "Ferguson has been an agent for decades. He was the director of National Intelligence. They admit he's crooked, it opens up a whole can of worms. Better to keep it in-house."

"Better to lie, you mean," I said, picking at the pepperoni on my pizza.

"Maybe on the news. But not where it matters," Black said. "We caught the weasel and his sidekicks. The truth prevailed."

"Because someone put a light on it," I said. Okay, so maybe I didn't get the words exactly right, but I got what Smith told me at the Lincoln Memorial. That fancy George Washington quote about the truth.

"That's right. You made a difference, kid." Black sat back in his chair. "All of you did."

"Well, I'm super happy that the mission was a success," Henry said, moving to slice seven in his pizza dinner.

"Affirmative," Ben said. He wiped his hands on a napkin and looked at Albert Black. "So where do we go for our next mission, sir?"

"We'll see, kid." Albert Black looked away.

"Let's just worry about getting you home, Linc," Stark said, her eyes dark. "You're leaving tomorrow first thing."

Home. Middle school, Racing Mania Eight, and spaghetti and meatball dinners. Now that sounded pretty perfect.

"No more missions for me," I said, raising my soda in a toast.

Ben smiled, and everyone tapped glasses.

Who needed secret agent life? Certainly not me.

Right?

EPILOGUE

TIME: A FEW WEEKS LATER

PLACE: MY DRIVEWAY

STATUS: CRAMMING STUFF IN THE BACK OF MOM'S VAN

"LINC!" MOM CALLED FROM THE PAS-senger side of the van.

"I'm right here, Mom," I answered from the back. "No need to yell." I was loading the hundredth dish in the trunk, on top of our bags and Grandpa's medicine box. "Why do we need to bring the whole house when we go visit Uncle Manny?"

Mom stuck bottles of water in the cup holders. "You know how your aunt never has enough dishes. And I like to cook with my own." She closed the door and moved to the trunk, where I was cramming paper plates in a corner. "Can you go see if Grandpa is ready to go?"

"Sure." I was happy to get out of packing-the-van duty.

"Make sure he wears his dentures. Last time, nobody understood a word he was saying."

I went inside, ready to deal with Grandpa and his teeth. I passed my backpack and board in the hall—it was still totally weird to think of that DC mission. The secrets, the whole saving the president thing.

Who was really behind Pandora? Were there more Dangerous Doubles out in the world?

Honestly, I didn't care. Agent Stark made good on her promise and got me a B-minus on my history test. We all got Presidential Medals of Freedom—mine was framed with a picture of me and President Griffin shaking hands after the private ceremony. I told Mom and Dad that I helped her catch a rat, which was pretty close to the truth. I had already leveled up twice on Racing Mania Nine. Life was good again, and I wanted to keep it that way.

"Grandpa?" I was about to go into his bedroom when the phone rang in the hallway.

Unknown caller. I picked up anyway, because I had that hunch.

"Linc," Black said in his deep voice. "I hear you're going to the City of Angels."

"Los Angeles, yeah," I whispered. "It's the annual family reunion and food fest." This was when the Bakers and extended family spent the weekend trying to impress one another with their cooking skills. "Why do you ask?" But I kind of knew.

"There's a case I want you on." Black coughed. "Couple hours of your day, tops. Happens to be right in LA."

"Lucky me. Why should I do this, exactly?"

"We'll tell you when you get there." And he hung up.

I should have called him back, told him to let Ben take the next case. But I needed to help Grandpa with his dentures. And Black said it was just a couple of hours, so how bad could it be, right?